Evilution

Elk Lake Publishing

Evilution, Episode 9

Copyright © 2014 by Ace Collins

Requests for information should be addressed to:

Elk Lake Publishing, Atlanta, GA 30024

ISBN-13 Number: 978-1-942513-77-3

Cover and graphics design: Anna M. O'Brien

Editing: Deb Haggerty

Cover Model: Alison Johnson Photography: Ace Collins

*Evil*ution

Ace Collins

In the President's Service Series: Episode 9

Elk Lake
PUBLISHING™

CHAPTER 1

Saturday, June 27, 1942
5:23 p.m.
Carfono's Warehouse located in
St. Louis Riverfront Slum District

Becca Bobbs glanced toward the warehouse Helen Meeker entered a few minutes before. *Come on! Something happened. Either get out of there or call us in!* Bobbs hated not to be in control, especially when a life was on the line. But hate it or not, she was stuck here in a wait mode.

Frustrated by what she didn't know, Bobbs turned her gaze to the two men guarding the gate. They appeared to be about forty and were dressed in brown uniforms with RC Furniture embroidered on the chest. The nearest one was about six foot tall and likely tipped the scales at two-twenty. The other, an olive-skinned man with cauliflower ears, was three inches shorter and at least fifty pounds lighter. As they leaned up against the chain link fence, they both looked as bored as she was trying to act. Did this pair know who they were really working for or were they just a couple of local stiffs who needed a job and took this one when it was offered? It likely didn't matter as these small fry could be handled pretty easily. If need be, she figured she could take them out by herself. But no one had ever been able to handle Carfono, and that was what really concerned her.

The book on Rudy said he was a man you never crossed; if you did, you died. But the mobster behind the hits was not the one Bobbs was most concerned about. She was wondering what kind of host Carfono was? There were a lot of hoods that were ruthless on the clock but were teddy bears in other situations. Was Rudy that way or did his lust for blood have no off switch? That dynamic, one the team, even with Vance's solid information, couldn't measure before the meeting, meant everything. So, was Carfono calmly listening and talking or was he looking for a way to punch Meeker's ticket to the next life? If only she knew.

Earlier in the afternoon, Bobbs had called on her long-forgotten high school acting skills to play the role of a cab driver and, by not missing a single shift on the ten-mile trip to this location, she had nailed it. Now, even as each of her senses was alive with anticipation and concern, the part she was playing demanded she act bored. So adjusting the cabbie's hat that rested on her reverse-rolled blonde hair, she stared into the taxi's rearview mirror and yawned. Yet even as she did her best to act disinterested, she remained in full observation mode. There were no cars coming up Riverfront Street. No one was walking down the street. Not even a bird was flying overhead. She frowned as she considered a line she'd heard a hundred times on radio shows and in movies, "It's too quiet." And now she fully understood what that could do to a person's nerves. She checked her watch for the eighth time in eight minutes. Come on!

After absent-mindedly tapping the Ford's large steering wheel, she reached into her purse. Her gun was there and she hoped it was going to stay there. She didn't itch for action because every time she'd had gotten into a gun battle, she'd lost someone she cared about and now there just weren't that many folks left to lose. Releasing her grip on the gun, she whispered, "Come on!" Though she'd thought it a dozen times since parking the car, it was the first time she'd said it out loud.

6

She might have been playing the part of a cabbie, but Clay Barnes drew a tougher assignment. He was hiding in the luggage compartment pretending to be a spare tire. Glancing to her left, she observed the other member of the team, Dizzy Vance, a rod and reel in hand, making a cast into the Mississippi River. As the man hadn't bought any bait, it was very unlikely he was going to catch anything. She figured both of the men were just as bored and likely just as nervous as she was.

Bobbs's blue eyes went back to the warehouse where Helen Meeker was playing a very dangerous game. Somewhere in that building, mobster Rudy Carfono was staring at a ghost. Bobbs was sure of that. After all, up until this afternoon, Carfono, just like the rest of the world, thought Meeker was dead. The press had overplayed the woman's tragic demise running story after story for four days. So while millions still bought into the lie that Meeker, along with Barnes and Bobbs, had met their demise in a plane crash, now the crime lord knew otherwise. How he was reacting to the beautiful ghost who walked and talked, as well as what kind of information he was giving Meeker, would likely determine if the team could save four handicapped friends of the president. No pressure there!

Now, stuck in a car with nothing but time, Bobbs really realized the whole case was screwy. It just made no sense. What did a bumbling spy caught by M16 have that was so important? Why would Hitler, who was fighting wars on two fronts, pay for the abduction of a quartet of polio victims in the United States just to try to convince the Allies to give Armstrong up? Even Himmler likely wasn't worth that risk. Then there was the question whether Nigel Armstrong was still alive or whether the Nazi bomb that destroyed OSS's secret facility also killed him? There were just too many questions and, sadly, none of them could likely be answered unless Carfono talked. And what were the odds of that happening?

"Come on," she whispered again while looking at her watch.

As Bobbs considered the worst case scenario—Carfono

pulling out a gun and shooting her friend—she grimly smiled at the paradox. She'd studied some law and, in this case, there was a unique legal precedent to consider. It would be hard to convict the mobster of murdering a ghost. After all, Helen Meeker was legally dead. Would that make this the perfect crime? She imagined herself a spectator in a courtroom. Carfono, dressed in an imported suit was sitting with his team of lawyers. One of them, a tall white-haired man with proper bearing, was showing a series of obituaries published in scores of different newspapers on the death of Helen Meeker. The attorney was asking, "How can you convict my client of killing a ghost? I mean do you believe in ghosts? Bobbs was still deeply lost in that irony, when, without warning, she was awakened from her daydream as all hell broke loose around her.

Sometimes explosions start with a rumble and build into a deafening roar. This one didn't. Suddenly St. Louis seemed to be on the war's front lines. With no notice, the warehouse groaned, windows rattled, and dust shot from the open roof. It didn't take a genius to realize something had gone terribly wrong.

It took Bobbs only a split second to grabbed her purse, toss it over her shoulder, find her revolver and throw open the driver's door. Meanwhile, Barnes, who popped the trunk lid and rolled out of the cab, immediately joined her. Confused but not confounded, both were poised and ready for action. The same could not be said for the two men who stood between Bobbs and Barnes and their objective.

The loud blast and shaking ground caught the astonished guards in such a state of shock they hadn't even considered reaching for their guns. Their faces now three shades lighter than they had been just a moment before, the slack-jawed pair whirled in unison and faced the building as the first signs of smoke began to pour from upstairs windows. Two seconds later, as they slowly turned back toward the taxi, Bobbs had them in her sights. Their lack of reaction answered one of the questions she'd asked herself earlier. As neither made a move for their weapons, these guys obviously weren't pros. This was likely their first rodeo and they'd just fallen off their ride.

"Drop the guns, boys," Bobbs barked as Barnes rushed around the guards and toward the warehouse. As she looked into the pair's shocked faces, Bobbs added, "And then raise those hands."

By the time their weapons hit the ground, Barnes was at the door and pointing his Smith & Wesson toward the blocky man who'd escorted Meeker inside. Barnes didn't bother asking any question before knocking the butt of his gun against the top of the man's head. Like air rushing out of a balloon, the man momentarily hovered before slowly spinning down to the ground. As the man crumpled, Barnes entered the warehouse.

"Okay, guys," Bobbs announced as she turned her full attention back to the guards, "you have a choice. Leave those guns where they are and get as far from this location as possible …" She raised her eyebrows and cracked, "… or I will be forced to shoot you both in the kneecaps. I hate to waste four bullets but, as I can't stay here and babysit you, I will if necessary."

The taller man glanced toward his companion before turning right and sprinting up the street. The smaller guard might have been a slower thinker, but he was a better athlete. He passed the big man within twenty yards. Bobbs was retrieving the discarded guns when a winded Vance jogged up to the scene.

"Take these," she ordered. "Then let's get inside and try to figure out just what happened."

"Whatever it was," Vance solemnly grumbled as she stuffed the two guns into his jacket pockets, "I can guarantee it's not good. That was a heck of a blast!"

By the time the pair reached the building, gunfire had broken out inside. Raising her weapon up beside her head, Bobbs cracked open and peeked in the door. About fifty feet to her left, Barnes, positioned behind an eight-foot high stack of two-by-fours, was taking on two very well-dressed gorillas armed with automatics and using roofing materials for cover. The odds were not in the good guy's favor. They grew even worse when he ran out of ammunition and had to stop and reload.

"You any kind of shot?" Vance asked as he studied the situation.

"Likely better than anyone within five miles of here," she whispered.

"Okay, then when we step in, you take the one on the left, and I'll get the one on the right. As we're not going to have any cover, I recommend you make sure of your first shot."

Bobbs nodded, took a deep breath, eased the door open and slipped in. She felt more than saw Vance follow. Without being noticed, they squeezed off two rounds almost simultaneously. The hoods, who likely believed they had the advantage over Barnes, and who had not anticipated the man having a backup, never knew what hit them. One of them fell backward into a stack of plywood while the other managed to stay on his feet just long enough to look toward Bobbs. After he had sized up the woman whose single shot caught him in the chest, he fell face down on the brick floor. No one had to check a pulse to know he was dead.

Rushing toward Barnes, who had now successfully reloaded and stepped from behind the wood, Bobbs and Vance scanned the rest of the large room. They appeared to be alone.

"What do you know?" the woman demanded.

"Nothing," Barnes admitted. "So let's move toward the place those goons seemed to be protecting. If we're going to find out anything, it has to be there."

Their heads on swivels and guns ready, the trio hurriedly jogged toward the back of the large building. Twenty seconds later they were at the base of a stairway leading to a second floor.

"What happened to all the smoke?" Barnes asked as he stood next to the steps.

"Based on my study of arson," Bobbs quickly explained, "I'd guess the fire's been contained to where the explosion erupted. Depending upon the type of bomb and combustible material around it, it might have even blown itself out."

"I don't care what happened to the smoke," Vance noted. "I just want to know where Carfono's other goons are. There have to be more. Rudy always has backups that backup the backups." Barnes peeped up the stairs. "I'm guessing Helen's up there and those goons we aren't seeing might be holding her."

"Nowhere else she could be," Vance noted, "that is if she's still in the building or even alive."

Ignoring the private investigator's morbid observation, Bobbs glanced up the stairs and then back toward the entrance. Once more things were much too quiet. As she turned to once again study the stairway, Barnes cautiously opened a door leading into another large room.

"You see anything?" the woman asked.

"There's a large door, big enough to drive a truck into, at the far end," he observed, "About all that's in there are two late model sedans and a decade-old Cadillac. Thankfully that room is fresh out of goons."

"Then," Bobbs suggested, "we go up the steps." After looking up the long flight a final time, she turned back to Vance. "Okay, Dizzy, you stay here and keep an eye on that door. If anyone comes in, then you have our tails."

"I have three guns," he explained, "so I can lay down a lot of lead. But if you hear me shooting, you get down here in a hurry. I'm not looking forward to dying alone."

"Good to know," Barnes cracked.

Bobbs nodded and, acting as the lead announced, "Clay, you and I are going up those stairs and finding out what's on the other side of that door."

"Good luck," Vance pronounced as he turned his gaze back toward the entry.

The woman grimly nodded and, with her gun aiming forward, raced up twenty steep wooden steps. Once at the top, Bobbs grabbed a deep breath and eased the door open with her foot. The room appeared as empty as a church on Tuesday.

While there were several desks, chairs, filing cabinets, and dust hovering in the air like fog, there were no people. Continuing to take in the eerie, almost surreal scene, she took a breath and noted a very strange odor.

"What's that?" Barnes asked.

"Plastic explosives," Bobbs whispered.

"How can you tell?"

"Trust me, I know what it smells like," she explained, "and I know how to use it too." The words had no more cleared her lips when three shots rang out. As she ducked behind a desk, she added, "I think we found the goons Vance was worried about."

Staying low, her gun ready, Bobbs crept forward toward an area where the smoke was denser. As she neared a partially open door, she heard another shot. This one seemed to have been fired from the right. Turning in that direction, she watched as a large man fell awkwardly out of the shadows to the floor.

Bobbs smiled. One prayer had been answered. They weren't fighting this battle alone. The mere fact the big man had just been shot meant Meeker was alive. But where was she?

"Helen," Bobbs yelled.

"Yeah." Came a calm reply.

"Are there any more?"

"Just one."

"Where?" Barnes demanded.

"Here." The stranger's voice was deep and accompanied by a body that would have had problems squeezing through a normal-sized door. As he emerged from the smoke, there was a strange look etched on his face—much like that of a college student trying to figure out the answer to a complex problem. The answer seemed to be eluding him.

As Bobbs turned and aimed, the man's puzzlement turned into a strange smile. With seemingly no reason, he lowered his gun, stumbled forward three steps and fell to his knees. After dropping his weapon to the floor, he glanced down at a white shirt that was fast becoming red, shook his head and made a grim observation. "Your friend's a good shot." He then tumbled face-first onto the wooden floor.

"Was that the last one?" Barnes asked a still unseen Meeker.

"Yeah," came the weak reply. A few seconds later, Meeker emerged from behind a partially opened door marked Private. She appeared dazed and was wobbling like a drunk as she moved forward. Her suit was torn and dirty; she sported scratches on her face and arms, but all that didn't matter at this moment. She was alive.

"What happened?" Barnes demanded as Bobbs put her weapon into her purse and hurried to help support the team leader.

"Get me out of here," Meeker demanded. "I don't want to be anywhere near this building when the cops and fire department arrive. I'm too tired to explain how a ghost can walk and talk."

With Bobbs supporting Meeker, Barnes led the way out the door and down the steps. After rejoining Vance at the base of the stairs, Barnes slipped his revolver into his belt and swept Meeker into his arms.

"Be best if I carry her," the man explained. "Let's get moving."

"May I suggest," Vance said, "that we take one of those cars." He pointed to the room. "I've done a bit of investigating. The old Caddy has gas, the keys are in the ignition, and that big door leads to an alley. I've already got it unlocked and ready to go up. I think we can get out that way much more quickly than going back to the cab."

"I'll lead the way," Bobbs announced as she again pulled out her gun. "Dizzy, you follow behind Clay."

The 1928 Caddy was huge and sported custom bodywork and a V-8 engine. As Bobbs opened the driver's door and slipped in behind the wheel, she noted the interior was plush and complete with a full bar. As the car's engine roared to life, Vance pulled a chain and opened the exit they were going to take. Meeker kind of fell out of Barnes' arms into the rear seat.

After racing around the back of the car, Barnes jumped in the other side. He'd no more than closed the rear door when the sound of machine gun fire filled the room.

"We've got company," Vance screamed as he hopped into the front seat.

"Hang on," Bobbs yelled as she hit the gas.

In spite of its age and weight, the green Caddy all but leaped forward, jumped out the door, and raced down the wooden ramp into the alley. Ignoring the gunfire that was now striking the rear of the car, Bobbs made a hard left and slammed the sedan into second.

"It everyone all right?" the driver asked as she accelerated and shifted to third.

"Yeah," Barnes answered. "The bullets hit the car and even the windows, but they just bounced off."

Vance laughed.

"What's so funny?" Bobbs demanded as she pulled the mechanical beast out of the alley onto a street and headed south.

The private eye grinned. "We just stole one of two bulletproof Caddies built for Al Capone."

Barnes shook his head, "And the Secret Service has the other one. I knew this car looked familiar."

"Thanks, Al," Bobbs whispered.

CHAPTER 2

Saturday, June 27, 1942
5:58 p.m.
St. Louis Riverfront Warehouse District

Al Capone's Cadillac was two miles away from Rudy Carfono's warehouse when Becca Bobbs met a police car, siren blasting, heading in the direction they'd just left. She observed the vehicle disappear in her rearview mirror before noting, "They'll be wondering why an empty cab is still sitting there."

"There's nothing to connect it with us," Vance assured her. "When I borrowed it, I didn't leave my name."

"Good to know," Barnes cracked.

After making a right leading away from the river, Bobbs glanced back into the mirror toward Meeker. It appeared as if she was having problems focusing. At times, her deep blue eyes appeared crossed.

"You all right, Helen?" Bobbs asked.

"I'm getting there," the woman announced. "The worst part of this is I'm seeing three Dizzies. The President didn't send us two more, did he?"

"There's only one of me," the investigator assured her.

An impatient Barnes ignored the cracks and demanded,

"What happened in there?"

Meeker shook her head. "Let's just say that Rudy will not be stealing any more gold. His forecast likely calls for lots of heat followed by even more heat."

"Dead?" Bobbs asked.

"Blown to kingdom come," the team leader assured her. "But he didn't make his exit before I found out Carfono didn't know anything about the abductions." Meeker stopped, took a deep breath, coughed some dust from her throat and continued. "He assured me kidnapping was not his game and I believed him."

Bobbs took another look in the rearview mirror to see if they were being followed. As she studied the thankfully tranquil scene out the back glass, she asked, "What about the explosion?"

Meeker shrugged. "The person who visited Carfono just before I arrived left an ugly black bag. I spotted it and handed it to Rudy. He informed me it belonged to a beautiful woman. He then carried the bag across the room and set it behind his desk. I'll bet dollars to donuts that purse was hiding a bomb. I heard a click and noted him looking down at the bag just before the explosion. Ironic that his final expression was one of confusion."

After making another right turn, Bobbs chimed in. "The bomb was likely made with plastic explosives, probably hidden in the base or the lining of the bag and rigged to a timer so the woman who left it could get away easily. That makes this a professional hit and a successful one at that."

"If he hadn't moved that purse behind his desk," Meeker said, wiping blood from her cheek, "The killer would have gotten two for the price of one. That huge hunk of antique wood saved my life."

Turning toward Meeker, Vance grimly smiled. "Having worked in Chicago and learned Carfono's operation, my guess is that someone within his own organization decided to remove Rudy from his position of power. If you're right about the bag being the bomb, then they got Carfono through his Achilles's heel—a beautiful woman."

"So," Bobbs cut in, "the crime syndicate's Samson got done in by a Delilah."

"That's my take," Vance added with a wry smile.

Barnes ignored Bobbs' touch of morbid humor and pushed the dialog back to a more serious vein. "Who benefits most by punching Carfono's ticket to hell?"

"Jim 'Jaws' O'Toole," Vance shot back. "And he has far fewer scruples than Carfono. He's from the Irish mob and is so ruthless he'd take out his own mother if she was trying to cut in on the mob's profits."

"So," Bobbs observed, "in the world of human sharks, we just traded a bad one for a really nasty fish."

From his spot in the front seat, Vance nodded grimly. "If this is O'Toole's work, you can expect a few more hits over the next month or so. Jaws will get rid of anyone who was loyal to Carfono. I predict the undertakers and the florist shops in St. Louis and Chicago are about to become very busy."

Shaking her head as if to clear the cobwebs, Meeker glanced up toward the driver and tried to push the conversation back toward the reason they'd made this trip. "What Jaws does is not our problem right now. We have four innocent folks we need to find and we just wasted a lot of time on this trip to St. Louis."

"Maybe not," Vance suggested.

"I tell you," Meeker hoarsely barked, "Carfono didn't do it."

"I'm not doubting that," the private investigator explained, "but I still hold that whoever's behind this is in the center of the spider's web. When you look at the four crimes, St. Louis is about as close to the center as you can get. We just need to reexamine our evidence and find someone else who fits the profile."

"So we don't leave the city?" Barnes asked.

"I'll do what Helen thinks best," Vance announced, "but I'd still bet on the man behind this mess being in this area."

"How are you feeling, Helen?" Bobbs asked as she again studied the woman's reflection in her rearview mirror.

"Better now," Meeker assured her friend. "The ringing in my ears is down to a low roar, the world's not spinning as fast as it was, and I'm down to seeing only two Dizzies. Except for some scrapes and bruises, I should be fine by tomorrow." She glanced up to find the driver's eyes in the mirror. "Becca, do we have all the case files with us?"

"They're on the plane," Bobbs assured the team leader.

"Okay, then I'm going to defer to Dizzy," Meeker announced. "Let's go back to the hanger. Let me get cleaned up and then we will reexamine the evidence. There has to be something we're missing. If we don't find it soon, then four others are going to meet the same fate as Carfono. I just don't think I could live with that."

Bobbs nodded, made two more right turns, entered Highway 66 and headed toward the private airport they were using on the outskirts of the city. This hadn't played out the way they'd planned but at least all them were still alive. So, for a change, using her gun hadn't also meant writing an obituary for someone she loved.

CHAPTER 3

Sunday, June 28, 1942
5:35 a.m.
8 miles west of Potsdam, Germany

Still dressed as Luftwaffe officers, a relaxed Reese and Holsclaw were driving a 1936 Mercedes west on a rural road toward the Netherlands and the safety at one of their hideouts. Armed with enough forged paperwork to likely get into the Reichstag, their main concern was time. They needed to get back to their headquarters as quickly as possible to arrange transport to England. Once across the channel, they'd join the search for the mysterious Nigel Armstrong—the one man who could reveal Holsclaw's role as the head of the Shadows of Night underground group.

Reese was seemingly more concerned about the missing spy than the Dutchman. In the time they'd worked together, the American had discerned that Holsclaw was somewhat of a fatalist. He seemed to understand the game he was playing could only go on for so long before the Germans showed up at the right place and the wrong time. When that happened, there would be no giving up; one side or the other would be dead. The Dutchman had beaten the odds long enough to figure his time was coming.

Reese was of a different bent. He understood the risks but never doubted his own ability to beat the devil. The fact that hundreds from the OSS and M16, as well many other civilian authorities, had failed to find Armstrong didn't matter. The former FBI agent just had a gut feeling he would uncover something the others had missed. As he mentally prepared for that job, he noted the Mercedes begin to lose speed. A glance forwarded revealed an unexpected checkpoint looming just ahead. As he approached the Gestapo-manned roadblock, the Dutchman glanced over to his American companion.

"What do you think this is all about?" Reese asked.

"Likely nothing we need to worry about," Holsclaw assured him as they grew closer to the armed men, "but have your weapon ready just in case. Based on what our headlights are showing, there are six of them, and as we have surprise on our side, we have a pretty good chance if we have to shoot our way out of here."

"You might like the odds," Reese noted, "but I don't."

As the large, open car rolled to a stop, a short, thin man flashed a light toward the vehicle's front seat. After studying their visitors' uniforms, he switched off the flash and barked. "Papers, please."

Wordlessly Holsclaw reached into his coat pocket, retrieved the paperwork, and handed the forged documents to the major. The officer flipped his light back on and scanned the papers before looking back into the car and asking, "You're Captain Bloom?"

"Yes. Now that we have proven you can read, what's this all about? Why is the Gestapo stopping Luftwaffe officers?"

The major glanced back to his men. That seemingly innocent look must have been a signal as immediately all five raised their weapons. So much for the odds favoring Reese and Holsclaw! Now secure in the knowledge his unit was ready for action, the Gestapo officer barked out an order.

"You will now get out of your vehicle."

"This is an outrage," Holsclaw protested. "Since when does the Gestapo tell the Luftwaffe what to do and where to go? Let us pass or you'll be spending the winter in Russia."

"Step out," came the strong command. "And don't try threatening me again."

"Himmler will hear about this," the Dutchman snarled as he pushed open the driver's door and exited the Mercedes. On the other side of the vehicle, Reese followed suit. Surprisingly no one moved forward to disarm them.

"Schmidt," the major snarled, "Search the car."

As a confused Reese watched, the German looked under seats, behind cushions, and even beneath the carpets. Only after popping the lid of the trunk and shining a light into every corner did the enlisted man march back to his commanding officer and issue his report.

"Nothing."

The major nodded, walked in front of the still running car and over to Reese. He silently studied the man as if he was examining a work of priceless art before asking, "What were you doing in Helga Smith's apartment?"

If the Gestapo didn't doubt Reese's and Holsclaw's false identities, this likely meant they'd somehow pegged Smith as a spy. As the former FBI agent attempted to devise a solid cover, the German tapped his holstered gun and again voiced the question.

"What were you doing in Helga Smith's apartment?"

"What does that matter to you?" Reese casually replied in flawless German. He remained calm and composed even though his pounding heart had leaped up into his throat.

"It doesn't matter to me," the major admitted, "but it does matter to Roderick Adelmann."

Another nail in their coffin! Someone must have seen them in Smith's hotel room. Did this mean the woman's cover was completely blown? That was a chilling thought.

"You are Kutz?" the major asked stepping closer to the American.

"I am," Reese replied trying to shape his tone to show he was growing tired of the major and his questions.

"What were you doing in Helga Smith's apartment?"

The American smiled. It was time to stall and there was no better way of doing it than by stepping on some toes. "I was an invited guest in her apartment. Why should that be a problem? Is Herr Adelmann jealous? I know I'm better looking than that old goat and likely a lot better conversationalist too."

The major spat at Reese's feet. "You pilots are so conceited. Do you think anyone in the Gestapo could be remotely jealous of you?" He stepped closer. "Now tell me why you were there?"

"My friendship with anyone is no business of yours," Reese shot back.

Before the major could counter, Holsclaw reentered the discussion. Unlike the American's combative verbal jabs, the Dutchman's tone was muted. "Tell them, Bruno. We have nothing to hide."

Reese nodded to his friend and then turned his eyes back to the major. "In spite of my friend's plea, I have no reason to tell you why we were there. By the way, I still don't think it's any or yours or," he paused for effect, "what was that other guy's name?"

"Adelmann."

"Herr Adelmann's concern," Reese smiled. "Who is this Adelmann?"

"At this moment," the major assured him, "he is your worst enemy."

"And I thought my worst enemies were the Spitfires and Mustangs flown by the Allied forces. I didn't know I was also fighting the Fatherland."

The major shook his head and growled, "I can take you back to Berlin and make matters very uncomfortable for you."

"Once again," Reese asked, as he glared down at the smaller

man, "Who is this Adelmann and why does he think my visit to Fraulein Smith is any of his concern?"

"He's the assistant to Himmler!" the major screamed.

"So, I ask you again, why is he interested in my visit with Fraulein Smith?"

"I don't have to give you the reason."

"Tell me, Major," a defiant Reese jabbed as he once again misdirected the conversation, "is Adelmann married?"

"Yes, he is."

"Does Smith work for the Gestapo?" the American countered.

"No, she doesn't."

Reese took a deep breath before he posed the question that might just open a dangerous can of worms.

"Major, is Miss Smith an enemy of the Fatherland?"

"No," came the swift reply.

That bridge hadn't blown up. So now he knew what the problem really was and could develop a story to fit those needs.

"Did Smith and Adelmann grow up together?" Reese demanded.

The German's blood was now obviously boiling. "Not that I'm aware of."

"Then, if Herr Adelmann is a happily married man, what difference does it make to him if Helga Smith spent some time with me?"

The major was evidently not used to anyone talking to him this way. His face was red, his eyes bulging, and he could have caught rainwater with his bottom lip. Wagging his finger, the black-clad officer yelled, "The Gestapo does not have to give you the reason we want to know something. Just tell me why you were with Smith?"

Reese grinned and casually gazed across the car to where a still calm Holsclaw was standing. "Captain Bloom, can you imagine why our visiting Helga could mean anything to the Gestapo?" The American laughed. "Is there something you're not telling me? Could you be a spy?"

The Dutchman grinned and shrugged.

How much longer was Reese going to yank his chain before giving the major an answer that might just satisfy Adelmann? At this moment, the game was so much fun the American didn't want to stop.

"Do you want to go to Berlin?" the major demanded.

"I was just there," Reese quickly countered, "I have no reason to want to go back. It's too much trouble dodging British bombs."

The German's chin dropped in apparent disbelief. His next question showed complete exasperation. "Then tell me why you were with Helga Smith?"

Reese set his jaw and defiantly demanded, "Tell me why you want to know?"

The major glanced back to his men, shook his head and frowned. As the Gestapo's officer expression transformed from indignation to acquiescence, it appeared that Reese's tactics had finally given him the upper hand. He'd pushed enough buttons and now it was time to see if the major would cave and tell them why their visit was so important to Roderick Adelmann. In the language of a gambling man, it was time to call.

"I'm waiting, major," Reese demanded.

His wait was a short one. The major moved close and whispered, "The matter is a delicate one. Let's just say that Fraulein Smith and Herr Adelmann are close."

Reese grinned. "So this is about jealousy."

"Yes," the major quietly admitted. "Now will you just tell me why did you visit her?"

Opting to get one more dig in, Reese smiled. "Would you shoot me if I confessed to having an affair with Helga?"

The major shook his head. "I hope I don't have to make that decision."

The American looked back to Holsclaw and grinned. It was apparent from his confused expression the Dutchman had no idea where the American was going.

"Her father was my pastor," Reese lied as he turned back to the major. "The fact is Helga and I grew up together. We're friends."

"No more than that?" the major demanded.

"No," the American assured him. "We had not seen each other for many years. As you likely are aware, in times of war, old friends become very important. When I was sent to Berlin, I decided to share with Helga what her father had meant to my life. I thought it might be the last time I'd have a chance to say those words. But I didn't kiss her. In fact, I didn't even touch her. So there's nothing for Herr Adelmann to be concerned about."

"You could have told me that when I first asked," the major suggested.

"You had no business asking," Reese snapped. "The Gestapo needs to be concerned about the underground and not with the Luftwaffe. I would guess there are likely members of the underground within spitting distance of us right now and you're taking up my time. Now, unlike you who to have time to spy on loyal Nazis, we have a job to do fighting the Brits and the Yanks. So can we move on?"

Seemingly satisfied, the major stepped back and signaled for his men to lift the barricade. As they did, Reese and Holsclaw slid back into the car, the Dutchman slipped it into gear, and the Mercedes lurched forward. It was a half a mile before either man was relaxed enough to talk.

"Why did you mock the major?" the Dutchman asked.

"You bully a bully," Reese explained. "Besides, if I had given him the information he wanted too quickly, he would have doubted us even more."

"Makes sense," Holsclaw admitted, "but I have a feeling your stall was more about trying to come up with a good story than it was running a tactical bluff."

Reese smiled. "Well, that was a part of it too. At least we didn't have to fight."

"And it sounds like we protected Helga too. So game, set, and match to the American."

"It's just a game," a suddenly solemn Reese replied. "We have a long way to go before we win a set or the match."

CHAPTER 4

Sunday, June 28, 1942
7:30 a.m.
A farmer's field outside of Burg, Germany

"Just not our day," Reese noted as Holsclaw slowed the Mercedes for the second time in two hours. At this rate, they were never going to get back to Holland to set up the trip to England. At least this time the roadblock was caused by something other than Gestapo swine.

Just ahead of their car, a farmer was pleading with a half dozen hogs. The pigs had somehow escaped their pen, were wallowing in the road and, the seemingly happy dark red hogs, were ignoring their owner. As the car pulled to a stop, the old man turned toward the supposed Luftwaffe officers and happily waved. He was either the friendliest man in the Reich or hoping to charm the two into helping him with this problem. Reese was betting on the latter.

"Those animals are too large to run over," the Dutchman grumbled, "and the fences are too close to the road drive around them."

"At least this is a higher class of animal," the American suggested, "than we dealt with earlier."

"Pigs are pigs," the underground leader cracked, "though, like you, I prefer this variety."

"Good morning," the farmer called out. "I'm so glad you're here. Been waiting for you all week."

That came from out of the blue. Why was a farmer looking forward to a planned visit from the German Air Force? As Reese silently attempted to sort things out, an equally surprised Holsclaw voiced his confusion.

"You've been looking for us?"

The winded old man ambled up the road, stopped in front of the Mercedes, put his booted foot on the bumper, and pointed toward a barn. "You'll find the plane over there. You can use my field to take off. It's long enough."

Glancing in the direction the man was pointing, Reese noted the tail of an aircraft visible behind the barn. With pigs in the road and a plane behind the barn, this had to be the strangest morning the American had ever experienced.

"I need to get rid of that thing," the farmer continued. "When it had engine trouble last week and they dropped it down on my farm, they took out a fence. That's why my pigs are out. And I'm still waiting on the government to pay me the money to fix it. They promised they'd do that."

Reese glanced down at what was likely the property line and noted a section of wooden fence that had been knocked down. While it appeared as though the farmer had tried to patch it with rusty chicken wire, the quick fix obviously hadn't worked. As the American stood up in the convertible to examine the damage more closely, the old man continued his story.

"I figured, last week when the mechanics came and got the plane's motors running, you people would be here immediately to fly this thing out. I also thought you'd have the money they promised so I could fix the damage that was done. I mean you can bomb London all you want, but I'd rather you not fight the war on my farm."

Holsclaw nodded and smiled as he stood, leaned close to

Reese, and whispered. "Do you want a faster ride?"

"Do you fly planes too?" Reese asked as he wondered what other skills the Dutchman had of which the American was unaware.

"I flew a few lightweight jobs before the war," Holsclaw assured him. "My older brother was a pilot for a mail service. He hopped between Holland and England on a regular basis. He was the one who taught me how to fly."

"I'm game if you are," Reese replied. "As my pappy always said, 'never look a gift pig in the mouth.'"

"How's that?" Holsclaw asked.

Reese waved and laughed, "I think there was something lost in the translation."

In truth, the American was more than ready to dump the Mercedes and all the problems traveling on the ground created. Besides, the aircraft might offer them more than just a ride back to their hideout in Holland; it also could give them an easier way to get to London and join in the search for Armstrong.

Holsclaw pulled the car into the lane leading to the barn. After shutting off the motor, he got out and led Reese and the farmer to the objective. As he closed in on the warbird, he was grinning like the cat that had just eaten the canary. When the trio rounded the corner of the building and really got a good look at the plane, the Dutchman cut loose with a riotous laugh.

"We just hit the jackpot," Holsclaw cackled just loud enough for Reese to hear. "Having one of these at my disposal is going to change the way we do business."

Reese glanced at the obviously confused farmer, who had evidently heard nothing, and shrugged. Yes, the twin-engine plane sitting in six-inch-high grass certainly appeared airworthy. The paint was faded, the lettering a bit weathered, but any damage created during its forced landing was not apparent. Best of all, it was well-armed. The American's eyes were fixed on the forward machine guns as a still excited Holsclaw quickly circled the plane.

"It's an early model of the Bf 110 Messerschmitt fighter," the Dutchman explained when he had taken a full three hundred and sixty-degree trek. "It has what we call a dachshund belly fuel tank."

Not knowing if that was good or bad, Reese nodded. In his view, the tank made the plane look pregnant. And as he couldn't remember seeing another one like it, he figured that feature must have been altered soon after the Bf 110 was designed.

"But will it fly?" the American asked when Holsclaw completed a second inspection walk around.

"It certainly isn't one of the best of the German warbirds," the Dutchman noted, "but it could still inflict some damage." He leaned close to Reese, "If it flies as well as it looks, it might even be our ticket to get to a place where we can look for that English spy."

"That's what I was hoping," Reese whispered back.

Perhaps figuring it best to grease a squeaky wheel, Holsclaw reached into his uniform's pocket and retrieved a wad of cash. "This should fix the fence and a few more things around here." After handing the bankroll to the farmer, he followed with a favor. "Could you store our car in your barn? We'll come back and retrieve it when we have a day off."

The old man, still marveling at the money he'd just been handed, nodded. "I will even wash it for you if you want."

"That won't be necessary," the Dutchman replied. "I think the mud gives it character. But please don't tell anyone you have it. I wouldn't want it falling into the hands of the underground."

"I promise," the man assured him. "After all, I am a loyal German."

"I'm sure you are," Holsclaw noted before looking toward his companion. "Let's get in and take this bird home."

Reese followed his partner to the Messerschmitt, hopped up on the wing and, as the Dutchman dropped into the front seat, the American slid into the second. While Holsclaw familiarized himself with the controls, the FBI agent watched the farmer stroll back to the lane, open a gate and hop into the Mercedes. The old man had just driven the car into the barn when the American noted the German equivalent of a jeep chugging down the road.

"We have company," Reese pointed out as Holsclaw seemed to be reaching forward with the intent of firing up the plane's engines. "Do we meet them or take off now?"

"Not enough time to take off," came the calm reply. "Based on what I'm seeing, we outrank them. So let's see what they need. Besides, if we tried to escape, they might just shoot us and damage our ride. Now that I've got this prize I want to keep it in good shape. Imagine the underground having a fighter that the Germans think is one of theirs!"

Three men in German Luftwaffe uniforms got out of the Kubelwagen and slowly walked down the lane in the direction of the barn. Two of them were carrying flight gear and parachutes. It didn't take a Rhodes Scholar to grasp that these were the guys assigned to bring the bird home. So this might get ugly in a hurry. In fact, it had the potential to become the Nazi equivalent of the Gunfight at the Okay Corral.

"I sure hope we're the Earps," Reese whispered.

"What?" Holsclaw shot back.

"Nothing."

"Henry," the Dutchman ordered more than suggested, "get out of the plane and take a place behind the far corner of the barn. Hurry! They aren't going to just hand this baby over to us, so we need an element of surprise. If they draw their guns and demand I get out, I'll pick off the one nearest me. It's your job to get the other two before they have a chance to shoot me."

There was no need to reply; the American now knew all he needed to know. Sliding down the wing on the far side of the plane, Reese hurried to his assigned spot. Once hidden, he watched and waited.

The Luftwaffe trio were casually chatting as they strolled toward the plane. The conversation abruptly stopped when they spotted Holsclaw. They eyed the stranger before a tall, thin man asked. "What is this?"

"Are you the pilot?" the Dutchman demanded in a very authoritative tone.

"Yes. I'm Willie Koffman. Who are you?"

Remaining in the plane Holsclaw barked, "Why weren't you here earlier?"

"We had to wait to get a car," Koffman explained.

"I've heard that line before," the Dutchman grumbled. "If we officers gave excuses like that to the Fuhrer, do you know what would happen?" He allowed his words to drift across the farmland before adding, "We'd get shipped to the Eastern front. And I've never actually talked to anyone who came back from Russia. Have you?"

Koffman ignored the question. "But why are you here?"

"Say 'sir' when you address me," Holsclaw demanded. "And I'm here inspecting the work done on this plane. We got word that one of the mechanics in this area was in league with the underground. I wanted to make sure this bird had not been sabotaged."

So far the ruse was working. For the moment, it appeared the trio was fully buying into the Dutchman's bluff. Still, Reese kept his weapon drawn and ready.

"May I ask your name?" Koffman inquired.

"Captain Bloom."

"Hans Bloom?"

"Yes," Holsclaw assured him.

With no warning, the young pilot reached for his sidearm. Seeing his actions, his two comrades followed suit. Surprisingly, the Dutchman didn't react.

"I know Captain Hans Bloom," Koffman noted. "In fact, he taught me to fly. He died three weeks ago. You're not Hans Bloom. So who are you?"

As he waited for Holsclaw to make the next move, Reese tensed for action. Noting that his friend was still staring at the Nazi's spokesman, the American set his sights on the small, stocky man standing just to Koffman's right.

"It would be best for you," the Dutchman slowly explained, "if you dropped those weapons."

"We have the advantage," Koffman pointed out with a smile.

Even if the trio couldn't see it, Reese knew that Holsclaw had his gun ready. The only question now to be answered was when he would shoot. As the seconds ticked by, the American watched the Dutchman study the three Nazis, his eyes flashing from one to another. Only when they locked once more onto Koffman did Reese know it was almost time for the fireworks to begin.

"Koffman," Holsclaw asked, "are you or any of your men married?"

"No," came the quick reply. "None of us is."

"That makes this easier," the Dutchman sadly announced. As his hand moved just above the edge of the cockpit, a shot rang out. A second later, Reese squeezed the trigger on his service revolver. Shifting at the same instant, the American and the underground leader aimed their weapons at the third man. Surprisingly, he was already falling forward, blood spurting from his mouth.

A stunned Reese glanced toward the barn. Standing in the doorway was the farmer. He held in his hands what looked to be a vintage World War I rifle. It was still smoking.

"I take it you aren't members of the Luftwaffe," the old man calmly declared.

"No," Holsclaw admitted from his position in the plane. "We're anything but Nazis. But how could you tell we weren't and they were?"

The farmer smiled. "You gave me money. The Nazis wouldn't have done that."

Reese made a note to remember that for future dealing with civilians.

"We've made a mess for you," the Dutchman announced as he stood and stepped out of the plane cockpit.

33

"Nothing I can't take care," the old man assured him. "I'll bury the bodies and put the Kubelwagen in the barn with your car. If this keeps up, I'll be able to open a used car lot."

"We don't want you taking risks for us," Holsclaw declared as he hopped off the wing and to the ground.

"No trouble at all," the farmer assured them. "But you might want to wait and let me remove the bomb I added to that metal bird. It would have blown up when you hit three thousand feet."

Reese looked to Holsclaw and back to the farmer. "You sabotaged the plane?"

"Ah," he laughed, "that's just the beginning of my work. I normally do much bigger jobs than that. Now let me disconnect the explosives so you boys can get out of here."

As the farmer opened up the right engine cover and went to work, Reese leaned over to Holsclaw. "Why did you ask the guy if any members of the trio were married?"

The Dutchman grimly smiled. "It might sound silly to you, but I just wanted to make sure I wasn't taking a father or husband way from his family. I mean, the enemy is the enemy, but there is still a part of me ..." His voice drifted off.

Reese nodded. He'd never thought of it that way. In his mind, the enemy was somehow less than human, and maybe men like Hitler were, but what about those three guys on the ground? They didn't ask for the war and they didn't wake up this morning thinking they would never see another sunset or have another date. In their minds, life likely stretched out forever. They had no idea death was one step behind them. But, as Holsclaw had noted, at least they didn't have kids.

Turning his attention back to the German plane, Reese found his voice and asked, "You sure you can fly this thing."

"No problem," the Dutchman guaranteed. "But if you want to grab the parachutes off those dead guys, I wouldn't refuse to put one on. And make sure they don't have holes in them."

"What about him?" Reese asked pointing to the farmer.

Holsclaw grinned. "He must be one of us. I know there's a

unit in this area and the men have taken out a couple of munitions trains. If we can find Armstrong and stop him from revealing my identity, I might just come back and bring this old man onto our team. I like his style."

Reese grinned. So did he.

CHAPTER 5

Monday, June 29, 1942
9:35 a.m.
FBI Headquarters, Washington, D.C.

In her first hour on the job, Leslie Bryant had been given the office tour and then handed a number of handwritten reports to type. She was now filing those reports just outside her new boss's door and it gave her the perfect vantage point to listen as the FBI's director exploded. In fact, Hoover's screams could likely be heard at the White House. The recipient of this fiery wrath was James Killpatrick. The agent was being dressed down to the point where he was figuratively naked. Though many people could hear the director's ear shattering performance, no one was enjoying it as much as the eavesdropping Bryant.

"Jim, you're an idiot. In fact, you're not just an idiot … you're a world-class idiot. I put this case in your hands and what did I get?" Hoover paused, likely trying to catch his breath, before launching another machine-gun-style verbal assault. "The man I wanted is dead before we even got the chance to talk to him. He is not just dead; he was blown to smithereens. How did you let this happen?"

As Bryant glanced through the two-inch crack in the not

quite closed door, she almost laughed out loud. Like a whipped dog, the now wounded Killpatrick ducked his eyes and shook his head. He shifted a bit in his chair before putting forth a timid rebuttable. "I didn't let anything happen. We were investigating Carfono, but we didn't have enough on the guy to haul him in. If we had arrested him, he would have been free in ten minutes and the agency would have been a laughing stock. I was just waiting to get the clue I needed."

Bryant shook her head. What a lie! Last night, during pillow talk, Killpatrick had admitted he was glad Carfono was gone because it protected some of his interests. The woman had a pretty good idea what that meant. Besides, Bauer had told her they were taking out Rudy for Killpatrick.

As Bryant continued to watch through the partially open door, a seething Hoover rose from behind his desk, pointed his stubby index finger right into Killpatrick's face, stopping only inches short of his nose, and screamed, "Jim! The guy who grabbed those cripples is dead. Do you get that? The one source we had for digging up the information is … let me spell it out for you … D … E … A … D. This really puts my rear on the line. When he finds out, the President's going to blow his top and I'm going to get blamed."

The director angrily pushed his hands into his suit pants and marched back around his desk. After taking a seat, he once more glared at his agent as he loudly barked, "Who killed Rudy? Do we have any lead on that?"

"No," Killpatrick admitted.

Bryant nodded. That was at least true. The agent had no idea she was the one who delivered the package that signed the mobster's death warrant.

"No clue at all?" the director grumbled.

The agent shrugged. "We're not completely in the dark. My theory is that it was someone inside the organization. After all, he had to be scared of something or someone or why else would he have moved from Chicago to St. Louis?"

"He was scared of us," Hoover shot back. "He's been nervous ever since the Fort Knox deal went south. That's why he moved. And that's why a few of his men who likely knew about that heist have been found dead. He was getting rid of everyone who might tie him to that case."

"But we didn't tie to him to it," Killpatrick argued. "And if his men who knew about it were dead, why would that cause him to fly?"

"He was scared of me," the director screamed. "This might surprise you, but a lot of people are." He lowered his voice and cracked, "I'm certain he wasn't trembling because of you. After all, Jimmy, you've been working on nailing Carfono for two years and you've tied him to absolutely nothing. We have more scandalous stuff on FDR than we do on one of the biggest dealers in vice in the world. Why is that?"

"I don't know," came the quick reply. "I mean, he's very good at covering his tracks."

"You're an idiot," the director repeated. "No one is that good. Give me a week and I can find dirt on a nun."

"I'm sorry, sir."

"Get out of here," Hoover barked as he pointed to the door, "and find those kidnapping victims." He paused and lowered his tone. "Jim, find them before someone kills them or your days here are numbered. Do you know what I mean?"

"Yes, sir," Killpatrick whispered as he got out of the chair, quickly buttoned his suit coat, pulled open the entry, and hurried from the room. The agent was obviously scared and the FBI's newest employee was enjoying it.

"Miss Bryant," Hoover called out. "Would you step in here for a moment?"

"Do I need to bring a notepad?" she asked.

"No," came the quick response, "just come in and close the door behind you. We need to talk."

Setting a file down on her desk, the woman stood, smoothed her green suit's tight skirt, strolled into the director's office, paused, pushed the door closed and waited. Other people would have been nervous while facing the nation's top cop, but Bryant was not like others. Having the director in a one-on-one conversation was just what she wanted.

"Have a seat," Hoover suggested pointing to the wooden chair Killpatrick had just vacated. After she was seated and had crossed her right leg over her left, letting the heel of her pump dangle just as it had in Carfono's office two days before, Bryant observed him eye her up as if measuring her for a suit. As the director continued his silent assessment, the woman looked around the room.

While much bigger than the other agent's digs, the office was not as large as she expected. A massive bookshelf stood on the left, an American flag was to the right and stood against a white wall. A few feet from that was a closet that sported double doors. The wooden desk appeared to be mahogany and was actually smaller than the one she'd been assigned. On the desk were files, an intercom, two brass lamps, a phone, a small sculpture serving as a penholder, and a legal pad filled with hastily scribbled notes.

The man sitting behind that desk in a large, thickly padded swivel chair was equally unimpressive. He was small, stocky, and unattractive. Dressed in a dark suit, white shirt, and blue tie, he looked more like a banker than a lawman. Only his jutting chin and foreboding, dark eyes gave him any character at all.

"Miss Bryant," he began, as he leaned forward in his chair and rested his elbows on his desk. "No doubt you heard what I said to Agent Killpatrick."

"Yes, sir."

"I want you to promise me," Hoover continued, "that what you heard will not get out of this office."

"Everything stays here," she quickly assured her new boss.

"I likely should have handled it better than I did," the man admitted, his bulldog jaw dropping a bit as he stood, turned, and walked over to a window. "I'm frustrated and when I get painted into a corner, I yell."

The raven-haired woman smiled. "Nothing wrong with that. From what I could gather, you had every right to get in the man's face."

Hoover glanced back to his guest and smiled. "I usually only voice my anger to my agents, so don't worry about my hitting you with something like that."

"If you do," she assured him, "I can take it."

The small man shrugged. "Your résumé is solid and, since I just lost an important member of my office staff, I can use your skills. So I don't want episodes like what you just witnessed run you off."

"They won't," she assured him. She paused while the director studied her every move, licked her lips and asked a question. "Might I make an observation?"

Hoover leaned back in his chair. "I have a few minutes, so what do you have for me?"

"You mentioned my résumé and I think it might offer me a way to help you right now." She could tell by the man's raised eyebrows that she'd caught his attention. Pausing, she considered the fabrications Bauer had written into her past. One of them now fit perfectly into this game she was playing and it was time to drop that card.

"When I worked at the *Chicago Tribune*," she began, knowing her lie was backed by that faked résumé, "I had the chance to go undercover as a woman of the evening. I did that to gain information on the mob. What I learned during that assignment now assures me Carfono had nothing to do with the kidnappings of those four people."

"What makes you say that?" a seemingly interested Hoover leaned forward and asked.

Much like a fisherman waiting for his prey to really get interested, she knew setting the hook too quickly might cost her the catch. So she opted to play this out very slowly.

"Are you sure you want to know?" Bryant asked. "I mean I'm just a woman, not a trained field agent. Maybe I'm just wasting your time."

"No," he assured her. "I want to hear what you know about Carfono." He sat back down at his desk and folded his arms. "Go ahead. Tell me why you think we've been barking up the wrong tree."

Satisfied she had his full attention, she leaned forward. "Rudy didn't like loose ends. There are way too many of those in the kidnapping racket. Therefore, it goes against his nature to get involved in something like that."

"You sound like you got to know the man really well," the director noted, hinting at a degree of admiration.

"I've looked him in the eye," she assured her new boss. She arched eyebrows before adding, "How do I put this ... let's just our relationship was explosive."

Bryant smiled as she considered her inside joke. Meanwhile Hoover, who normally had little use for a woman, had, for the moment, fallen under her spell. Proving he wanted the conversation to continue, he put his arms on his desk and posed another question.

"If you knew Carfono so well, and you're sure he didn't do it, then do you have any idea who did?"

"At this time," she admitted, "I don't. But I can put an old source on the case and see what he digs up. That's up to you."

"We can't have the press getting wind of this," Hoover warned with a wave of his left hand. "The press fouls things up. I use them when needed but otherwise keep them in the dark.

The woman nodded. "My source doesn't like the press or the police. Let's say that my source is on the dark side of the street and he doesn't want the power turned on there."

"So no publicity," Hoover noted.

"None."

"But how ..."

She cut him off. "He owes me some favors. In fact, a lot of people owe me favors. How do I explain this?" She paused and allowed a seductive smile to set the tone for the words that followed. "I was born both beautiful and smart. When I put those two together, I find they work magic in a man's world. I can pretty much dial up any number I want and get an answer. Do you understand what I mean?"

He nodded and posed a very interesting question. "Then why work here?"

It was time to justify her actions to a man known to be a moralist. "We're in a war and there are ways my skills can be used to help this country as well help myself."

"What's in it for you here at the FBI?" he softly but forcefully demanded.

"Let's just say I will get to know some very important people as I work for you. After the war, those people could help me get a few things I want in life."

He shook his head. "What makes you think I need someone with your gifts?"

"The president wants those crippled folks back," she noted.

"So do I," he cut in.

Bryant's face grew dead serious. "You told Killpatrick your tail was on the line. That's not good for you and it's not good for those who work for you and that includes me. So here's my offer: if I deliver those people safe and sound to you, will that prove you need someone like me here?"

Hoover rubbed his chin and frowned as he considered his newest employee's rather dark offer. She wondered if she'd overplayed her hand. Perhaps she shouldn't have exposed as much of her apparent willing nature as she did.

"Miss Bryant," the director finally replied, "I demand my agents follow a very high moral code."

She grinned. "Mr. Hoover, I know that but what do you demand of someone like me? I'm not an agent. I'm just a beautiful woman with twice the brains of James Killpatrick."

He shrugged.

"Mr. Hoover, I'm not trying to seduce you. I know you're not interested in what I have to offer on a personal basis. But there are others who look at me in another way. I can crack most men's high moral standards like a squirrel cracks a peanut. I'll admit that I'm not what you would call a good girl and I don't mind you knowing that. In fact, you need to know it."

"Miss Bryant," the director cut in, "I'm not sure where you're going. In fact, I'm not even sure I want to know where you're going."

"Mr. Hoover," the woman cooed, "rumor has it you have a file on every important person in this country. When the time is right, you use the dark stuff in those files to get what you want. I can add a few chapters to your files that will prove very beneficial down the line."

Hoover licked his lips but didn't really address what Bryant had just said as he picked up the conversation. "So you think you can find the victims that are being held in this kidnapping deal?"

"I have a much better chance than Killpatrick does," she confidently noted.

He raised his eyebrows as he lowered his voice. "You get me some real information on the kidnappings and I will consider if we can use you in other areas. Until then, you're a file clerk."

"I understand," she answered. "I'll put my source to work on the case."

She then smiled, uncrossed her legs, opened the door, and slowly exited the room. For the moment, she was satisfied to work for Hoover, but someday she vowed to own him just like she owned Killpatrick, Bauer, and so many others. After all, it was in ownership where the real power was found.

CHAPTER 6

Monday, June 29, 1942
10:35 a.m.
A hanger at private airport ten miles outside of St. Louis

Dressed in a blue, button-up blouse, gray slacks, and sneakers, Helen Meeker, her arms crossed and her right foot tapping, stood in one corner of the small airplane hanger her team was using as a mobile headquarters. Though her scrapes and bruises gave evidence of her recent close brush with death, a couple of nights sleep had at least put her in a position to begin to feel like herself again. In other words, she was feisty and eager for action. Picking up a donut from a table, she walked back over to where a map was pinned to the wall. The location of each kidnapping was circled in red.

"Des Moines, Muncie, Chattanooga, and Tulsa," she announced before biting into the pastry. Only after finishing the donut and taking a sip from a six-ounce bottle of Coca-Cola did she add, "And we are about as close to the middle of that circle as we can be and still be in a major city. So, if the man in charge is in St. Louis, where do we find him?"

Dressed in one of his new suits, this one dark blue, Dizzy Vance leaned against the wing of the team's black DC-2 and stated the obvious. "We're either missing something that each of these cases has in common or we are way off the trail."

"What could we be missing?" Bobbs demanded while sitting in a chair just to Meeker's right. After adjusting her blue slacks and playing with the collar of her pullover summer sweater, she again listed off the facts. "Each victim had a known relationship with the President, but, even though they all visited Warm Springs, it appears none of them actually knew the others. We also know that their lives were tough but dissimilar, their ages varied, and they were each kidnapped by well-dressed, well-spoken men who drove nice but nondescript cars. Other than that, what do we have?"

"Nothing," Barnes grumbled from his position by the plane's nose.

Bobbs frowned as she mournfully announced, "The folks who build plane parts at Macomb Manufacturing likely know as much as we do. And their only source of information comes from stories penned for the Tulsa newspaper. We're busted."

Meeker snapped her fingers. "What are the odds?"

"What do you mean?" Vance asked.

"Mrs. Reason," Meeker explained, "mentioned a Macomb plant in Chattanooga too."

"I know the company," Barnes chimed in. "I did some research on them when they pledged to convert to production for the lease-lend program. I met the owner, his name was ... let me see ... oh, yeah ... Harold Schmeidler." After snapping his fingers, the man continued, "I hadn't thought about this for more than a year, but it's all coming back to me now."

"What difference does any of this make," Bobbs grumbled.

"Nothing," Barnes shot back, "but at least I have some facts I can spit out rather than just firing blanks."

"What about Schmeidler?" a disinterested Vance asked. "What made him so special you needed to work up a file on him?"

"Well," Barnes continued, "the man started his business in

the late twenties with one plant making kitchen furnishings and fixtures and then expanded from there. Somewhere in the early thirties, he purchased a couple of other industrial operations and then things really started to go right for him. He's literally into everything now. In fact, he has plants all over the country, but the company's headquarters is right here in St. Louis."

"Do all his plants operate under the Macomb name?" Meeker asked.

"No," Barnes replied. "That was a part of the research that drove me crazy. If they'd all had the same names, it would have been a piece of cake. But as he acquired other companies, he felt it was best to keep the original names and put them all under the umbrella of Harold Industrial."

"Why the first name?" Bobbs asked. "Most folks use their last names when creating an industry."

Barnes nodded. "Most do, but he thought many Americans would not be very comfortable with companies that didn't have American sounding names and he didn't want folks to think that his company was owned by Germans."

Vance, his face now revealing a lot more interest, pushed off the wing and ambled over to study the map. After a few seconds, he turned back to Barnes. "Schmeidler doesn't happen to own Hammond Manufacturing, does he?"

Meeker's eyes went hopefully toward Barnes. Maybe they had just stumbled upon the key to this series of crimes.

"I don't know," Barnes replied. "There were like a half dozen companies listed and I can't remember all of them now. I do recall that one was Thomas Electric."

"There are seven," a seemingly impatient Bobbs called as she studied a listing in a phone book. "There's an ad in the back of this directory. Here is all you need to know and then we can move back to the case at hand. Harold Industrial runs plants in fifteen different locations across the Midwest and South. Their names are Harold, Macomb, Johnson Plumbing, Thomas Electric, Radisson Industries, Dynamic Motorworks, Nichols

Rubber, and Hammond Manufacturing."

"There's a Hammond plant in Des Moines," Meeker chimed in. "I actually went into their offices to get change for the phone."

Vance stuck his hands in his pants pocket. "Hammond is where Madge Crawford worked." He grimly smiled and added, "I think we just connected the dots."

The hanger went silent as each member of the quartet considered the new evidence. Obviously the "go to" person on this was the man who'd already done the research. Unable to come up with a motive of her own, Meeker looked over to Barnes.

"Why would Harold Schmeidler be involved in this?"

Barnes moved from the plane over to the map where he joined the other three. "There is only one logical explanation. Schmeidler was born in Germany. That's why the Secret Service did the background check on him. We had to be sure he was on our side before we allowed him to meet with the President. Our research showed he emigrated in the early twenties and had immediately immersed himself in American life, so we had no concerns. But maybe we missed something."

"Let's make an appointment to see him today," Meeker suggested. "Let's find out just what you missed."

"I've got the number right here," Bobbs replied holding up the phone book. "I'll make that call."

After going through a switchboard operator and a secretary, Bobbs was on the line with Schmeidler's office.

"My name is Rebecca Roberts," Bobbs announced, falling into her cover identity. "I'm a part of a team from President Roosevelt's office and we need to meet with Harold Schmeidler as soon as possible."

As the other looked on, the blonde listened to the response and then countered with a lie. "I understand how busy he is, but this involves war production at his plants and is most urgent."

Meeker quietly moved toward Bobbs during the conversation's lull. As she grew closer, the team could now clearly hear the woman's voice on the other end of the line. "He's out of town right now but will be in tomorrow." "What time can we schedule a meeting?" Bobbs asked. "He usually gets here around eight."

Bobbs looked to the team leader. Meeker nodded. "We will be there first thing in the morning. Thank you."

Meeker quietly studied the map. Was this another blind alley or had they happened upon the lead they really needed? She needed to be prepared and they had less than a day to do the research and properly set the trap.

"Okay, gang," Meeker announced, "We'll all drive down to the plant, but I'd rather have just Becca and me go in. Schmeidler will likely underestimate two women. So we females have a better chance of catching him off guard. Meanwhile you men can take a gander at the plant and see if you can sniff anything out there."

"We might finally be onto something," Vance cracked.

"Yeah, maybe," Meeker agreed, "but before I meet him, I need to find out everything we can on this guy. I want to know how much he's worth, where he eats and, if he has a tattoo, I want to know what it says and where it is."

"I'll get Alison digging in Washington," Bobbs volunteered.

"I'm off to public records and the courthouse," Vance announced. "I'll have to use the Caddy to get there."

"Let me join you," Barnes suggested. "While you're going through the stuff that's on file, I'll take the car out to where he lives and question his neighbors."

"Call me," Meeker ordered, "if you get anything we can use."

As the men headed out the door and Bobbs placed the call to Washington, Meeker once more crossed her arms. This might just be another dead end, but if it wasn't and Schmeidler was behind the kidnappings, then that likely meant the parts he was manufacturing for the war effort could be faulty as well. If that was the case, it was time to shut this guy down and stick him in a prison cell and she was looking forward to being the woman who did that.

CHAPTER 7

Monday, June 29, 1942
7:35 p.m.
A small farmhouse four miles
southwest of Hengelo, Netherlands

The borrowed Bf 110 Messerschmitt was safely tucked away in a barn and its pilot and passenger had removed the Luftwaffe uniforms and were back in civilian attire. After eating a meal consisting of boiled potatoes and sausage, the Dutchman contacted London while the American took paint and brush and added a few white squares to the German plane's nose and twin tail. He'd just finished his work when the radio communication ended.

"Are we on?" Reese asked.

"The OSS and M16 are looking forward to our visit," a happy Holsclaw explained. "The code book we lifted a couple of weeks ago as well as some of the fortifications I noted on our trip to Berlin are going to be very welcome. As far as Armstrong is concerned, there are no updates."

Standing a bit away from the plane Reese grinned. "Hans, do you like what I've added to the fighter?"

The Dutchman nodded. "It's just as I described it to London.

They've alerted all the Allied fighters to be looking for those white boxes. I also gave them our projected flight path. They should intercept us over the channel and escort us to a base just north of London. The fact the plane still sports all its German identification should make this a smooth trip across Holland as well. Hence, no one will be shooting at us for a change. I kind of welcome that too."

"What about fuel?" the American chimed in. "The tanks were pretty low when we landed this crate."

"My men have a truck filled with barrels of aviation fuel on the way. It should be here within the hour. I figured we would pull the fighter out of the barn about eleven, load up, and take off. Just before we leave, I'll alert England so they will be looking for us."

"It all sounds so simple," Reese noted. "Just like getting on a TWA flight."

Holsclaw grimly smiled. "Much simpler than the ways we normally have to use to get back to England, but hardly like a commercial airline. Three people lost their lives for us to get this ride. That's a pretty steep ticket price."

The America didn't answer. There was really nothing to say. He had learned war was anything but glamorous. Instead, it was an insane exercise allowing men to use the latest technology for barbaric ends. Death, which made such a profound impact during times of peace, now was almost meaningless. If a few hundred or even few thousand folks were killed in battle, another group took their place and the bloodletting continued. If you thought about it too much, your mind went numb.

Holsclaw got up from the table and looked out the window of the barn. As he studied the cattle feeding in the meadow, he posed a question. It was likely just his way of passing the time, but in reality it also asked his friend to evaluate his own conscience.

"You asked me why I wanted to know if those Germans had children. Now I have to ask you something. Do you ever think about the men you kill?"

"I try not to," Reese admitted. "Whenever those thoughts crowd into my mind, I think of Betty Grable or Carole Landis."

"That doesn't work for me," Holsclaw sadly replied. "In fact, sleep is getting harder and harder."

Not wanting to admit he'd been thinking many of the same thoughts, the American pushed out a tried and true rationalization for the killing. "Hey, we didn't start this, we're just players."

"Most of them are just like us," the Dutchman noted.

"Who?"

"The Germans," Holsclaw explained. "They aren't bloodthirsty mongrels. They're just men with families, hopes, and dreams. The war put everything on hold for them. Suddenly what was unthinkable became the norm and everything they'd been taught that was morally wrong became acceptable."

"Like Helga," the American frowned as he offered the example.

"Yeah," the other man agreed as the barn again fell silent.

Smith was knowingly tossing herself into the gutter to help the war effort. She would have likely never even considered that in times of peace. Did that make what she did right at this moment but wrong the day after the last shot was fired? It was a question Reese wanted answered.

"Hans," Reese announced. "When this whole mess is over, if we live through it and our side wins, we will be hailed as heroes. But what will they call Helga? You and I will be responsible for hundreds of young men dying and yet she, who will likely never kill anyone, will still be scorned and ridiculed. She will carry a big red 'A' for the rest of her life."

"A red 'A'?" a confused Holsclaw asked as he turned back from the window.

The American shrugged. "Just a reference to a novel written by a man named Hawthorne."

"I see," the older man replied. He took a deep, almost mournful breath and added. "I wouldn't worry too much about

Helga."

"Why not?"

"Because she won't survive the war. Someone will find out what she's doing. She'll die at the hands of a firing squad or worse. And no one will ever know what she did to help our side."

That sobering thought forced Reese out of his chair. Shaking his head, he stood by a window and solemnly studied the sun setting across the meadow.

"Hans," he noted, "we have a license to kill. If Germans started walking across that piece of grass, we could step up and mow them down. When the war's over, the same people who gave us that license to kill will revoke it." He turned back to his friend. "How hard will it be for us to give it up? How hard will it be for millions of fighting men to suddenly quit solving disputes with guns and instead use words? How can lasting peace come from an orgy of bloodshed?"

Holsclaw shrugged. "Maybe, my friend, the lucky ones die rather than trying to rationalize what they've done or trying to once again answer disputes with words rather than bullets and bombs." His stinging words hung in the air, almost haunting the room, before the man quietly added, "Let's get cleaned up and have some coffee. It's going to be a long night."

Reese nodded. Maybe every night for the rest of his life would be haunted and long.

"What's the matter my friend?" the Dutchman asked. "It is Helga? She knew what she was getting into."

The American shook his head. "Yeah, I wish I'd never met her. And I wish ..."

"Wish what?"

"I wish you hadn't asked those men if they were married. That made this all too real."

"Henry, it is real and everyone needs to know just how real. If we survive this, let's make sure and tell them."

CHAPTER 8

Monday, June 29, 1942
11:35 p.m.
On a farm outside of Springfield, Illinois

Fredrick Bauer eased the phone into its base and frowned. After a full weekend of work, he'd managed just one small lead that he could pass along to Teresa Bryant and she'd already given that to J. Edgar Hoover. Unlike Killpatrick, he had feared Carfono was not behind the kidnappings. So rubbing out the mobster had really been a worthless act. Yet, if the mob wasn't working with Hitler, then who was? That led to the most troubling question of all. Why hadn't Himmler come to Bauer for the job? This was his kind of operation. And if they weren't going to use him, why hadn't he at least been told about it?

A day's worth of phone calls led to uncovering just two small scraps of information. One of Bauer's SS sources in Detroit indicated the kidnapping plot had been hatched in Himmler's office. He also shared that employing the American side of the operation didn't include any exchange of money. That had to mean the Nazis had a network in America Bauer did not know about. Where was it and who was running it?

The ringing of his desk phone drew his attention away from the problem of who, why, and where and pushed his mind back into the now. Bryant and two German agents knew this number. Carfono had too, but he was not likely to be able to make a call from where he was now. So who was on the other end of the line?

"Hello," the tall man cautiously announced as he drew the receiver up to his mouth.

"Is this the man known as Darkness?"

Bauer paused. Darkness was the code name he'd used when dealing with Carfono. To his knowledge, the mobster had never shared it with anyone else. So with Carfono dead, who was on the other end of the line and how had they gotten this number?

"Who are you?" Bauer hesitantly asked as he came back on the line.

"Don't you know?"

"Would I ask if I did?"

"Jaws," the man announced with what sounded like a bit of pride.

Bauer smiled. He now understood who the caller was and how he'd likely gotten the number.

Jaws O'Toole, the next in line to the crime throne, was not wasting any time shoring up his contacts. In a sense, that was good. This saved Bauer the trouble of introducing his services to the Irishman. Still, how much did he know about the operation? Rather than march blindly into a situation he was unsure of, Bauer opted to play a game.

"Am I supposed to know who Jaws is?"

"I think you know," came the quick response.

"Perhaps," Bauer suggested, "as you are the one who made the call, you need to enlighten me."

The line went mute for almost thirty seconds and during that time Bauer considered his options. If O'Toole knew the number, he likely knew the jobs he'd done for Carfono. If that was the case then that probably already had proven his value to the organization. But could the new man in charge have connected Carfono's death to Teresa Bryant? If that was the case, this might mean trouble.

"Does the name O'Toole mean anything to you?" the voice finally asked.

"There are lots of O'Tooles," Bauer noted.

"Only one who is now in the used furniture business," came the quick explanation.

The man was playing it smart. He was not giving away anything. That proved he'd learned a lot from Carfono. That indicated growth. Still what was the reason for the call? Bauer sensed the best way to find out was just to continue the game.

"I really don't need any furniture right now."

"We are little low on our stock anyway," O'Toole admitted. "This call was more about letting you know the business was now under new management."

"That's good to know," Bauer assured. "In fact, I'd heard that the old manager had unexpectedly been transferred."

"It was time for that move," O'Toole announced without emotion.

"Jaws? I believe that is what you said you wanted to be called."

"That will do for now."

"I'm surprised you had my number."

"There is a file," O'Toole explained, "It was written in a code that only Rudy and I knew. It was locked in a safe. I have that file in my hand and it contains a list of ... how shall I say this ... transactions that were exchanged between you and him. I was especially impressed with the way your company made Eddie Vettori disappear. Houdini would have not been able to duplicate that kind of magic."

"Who is this Vettori?" Bauer asked.

"You knew him as well as Lorch, DeVoss, and Colonna. And though I don't know how you managed to rid the world of those pests, I admit to being impressed."

Bauer smiled. The world was better off without those men, but that's not why he'd agreed to take on the task of booking their passage across the Jordan. He'd done it in exchange for favors Carfono had done for him. So where did O'Toole expect to take this now?

"Mr. Darkness," the voice on the other end of the line announced.

"My, aren't you being formal?" Bauer quipped.

"I need to know something."

"And what is that?"

"Does your contract still apply with the change in management?"

This was a positive note. It appeared O'Toole needed him. Still, this wasn't the moment to appear eager.

"That depends," Bauer explained. "Rudy and I had a mutual trust for each other. You and I have no history and, therefore, we have no grounds for real trust."

"Then we need to meet," O'Toole suggested.

"Why is that so important to you?"

"I need a man like you. There are times that things should be handled outside the organization."

Bauer smiled. He'd been worried about taking out Carfono. He figured it might take months or even years to groom O'Toole. But the unpredictable Irishman was already knocking on his door and offering a partnership of sorts. So finding out what he needed would likely be worth the time. Still, he wasn't going to cut the deal too quickly.

"I'm very particular about who I work with."

"Let's meet," O'Toole suggested.

"I'll think about it," came the quick reply.

"Darkness," the caller whispered, "I heard from a woman today who claims she knows who you are. She didn't give me your location but assured me she could. As you consider if we need to work together, think about that."

The line went dead.

The color drained from Bauer's face. The woman had to be Bryant and she was already playing him again. Finding out who she really was and where she came from now had to trump everything else in his world. At this point nothing else mattered. As he considered what his next move should be, a voice he'd never expected to hear shook him like a tornadic wind.

"You look worried."

A startled Bauer jerked his head toward the room's entry. Standing in the doorway was a ghost. It had to be. After all, the visitor had been written off as dead at least four times.

"Fister," Bauer whispered.

"Glad you remember me."

CHAPTER 9

Tuesday, June 30, 1942
12:02 a.m.
On a farm outside of Springfield, Illinois

"How?" Bauer's words hung in the air as his haggard guest eased down into a chair.

"No thanks to you," the visitor announced.

A still stunned Bauer uneasily studied the man sitting ten feet in front of him. Fister was thin, a week past due for a shave. His uncombed hair looked as if it was styled by a Kansas twister, his shirt was dirty, and his pants torn. He also appeared about fifteen pounds under his normal weight. Thus, this was hardly the superman Bauer had used his lab to create. But even though he was talking and even though he could hear his breathing, Fister couldn't be alive!

"My sources told me you were dead," a disbelieving Bauer noted. "And my sources are pretty good. The FBI even confirmed it. You cashed it in while staying at the loony bin. If fact, I celebrated your death with a steak and apple pie."

The visitor shrugged. "Maybe I am dead. I honestly feel more dead than alive. In truth, I can barely remember the past month of my life."

"What do you recall about New Orleans?" Bauer demanded.

"Wild town," came the quick reply. "There were some crazy people there too. By the way, did Meeker croak? I opted to allow a rather large gator to gorge himself on that dame."

"No," Bauer admitted, "she seems to have a knack for pulling herself out of death's jaws." The tall man leaned across his desk to get a closer look into the visitor's bloodshot eyes. "When was the last time you had a seizure?"

"Not in the last week or so."

"That's good. I need to check a few others things if you don't mind."

"Sure."

Bauer got up, grabbed his medical bag, retrieved his stethoscope and approached Fister. The man sat perfectly still during the two minutes of probing and prodding. Only after Bauer returned to his desk did the visitor again speak.

"Am I alive or did I die somewhere along the way and no one told me?"

"You could obviously use a few meals and some rest, but, all things considered, you're in pretty good shape."

"You say that like you're surprised."

"Shocked would be a better word," Bauer explained. "That water you drank in New Orleans was anything but the fountain of youth. The Corelles actually used it to drive people crazy."

"It must have worked for a while," Fister wearily replied, "but I think it wore off."

"No," Bauer cut in, "it doesn't wear off. Those who drink it go stark raving mad and stay that way. Just, as I understand it, you did. And none of them every returned from that bad trip."

"Well," the visitor cracked, "I'm not mad and I came back, so I got over it."

Bauer nodded. It appeared he had done just that. But how? Everything he'd learned about the water since returning from New Orleans indicated the stuff was lethal. So why hadn't it killed Fister?

"Could I have something to eat and a place to sleep?" the visitor asked.

"I guess so," Bauer replied as he turned his gaze from the man who'd once been his prize project to study a landscape of post-World War I Berlin hanging on a far wall. He allowed an uncomfortable silence to cloud the room before noting, "You know I should kill you for what you did in Louisiana."

"Fine," Fister sighed, "that would save you some food."

"Let's not go there now," Bauer suggested.

"So do I get to eat?"

"For the time being, I guess you can stay here. Feel free to go into the kitchen and see what you can find. I'll take care of a few things here and then we'll go over to the lab."

With Bauer watching his every move, the visitor slowly pushed out of the chair and staggered from the room. In truth, he did deserve to die. Bauer had killed men for doing far less than Fister and, at this point, ending his miserable life would be an easy task. Still with Bryant apparently going rogue perhaps this unexpected turn of events might come in handy. If he could get Fister back to fighting weight and restore a bit of his passion, then perhaps he'd be able to use the man to either control or take out Bryant. Yet, before that could happen, there had to be a restoration of trust. Thus, for the next few days, Fister would be locked in a room in the lab and closely observed. Bauer smiled, it was good to once again have a man's fate in his hands.

CHAPTER 10

Tuesday, June 30, 1942
8:33 a.m.
Harold Industrial Headquarters, St. Louis, Missouri

Forty-seven-year-old Harold Schmeidler looked nothing like a spy. He was barely five and half feet tall, might have tipped the scales at one-thirty and wore thick, Coke bottle-like glasses. This was the kind of man who had sand kicked in his face on the beach. His voice matched his body. If he'd sung in the choir, he'd have been a weak tenor. His handshake, though firm, was not one that would cause anyone to grimace. So, based on their initial meeting, it appeared like Meeker and her team had guessed wrong again. Still, after making the appointment and the trip into the man's office, the woman figured she needed make sure there was a not a snake with a lethal bite below the unimposing exterior. After all, J. Edgar Hoover was not exactly an imposing figure either and he could be deadly.

After their introductions, Schmeidler pointed to a couple of chairs and suggested everyone get comfortable. Then, with a smile he announced, "My secretary tells me you two are from the White House."

Before answering, Meeker surveyed the room. Not only was their host unimpressive, so were his digs. The office was about the size usually reserved for a foreman, not a CEO. The furniture was basic, the bookshelves lined with technical journals, trade publications, and the complete works of Mark Twain. An unopened morning edition of *The St. Louis Star* sat on the man's desk and a half empty water cooler stood in the corner. From what Barnes had discovered, the man's home was equally unassuming. So, for a rich man, Schmeidler appeared to live rather modestly or at least didn't want to show off the trappings of a millionaire and, in the way most wealthy American's liked to live large, that was strange.

"My name's Helen Miller," Meeker finally announced as she turned her eyes back to the host. Still working to catch the man off guard, she employed a stern but non-threatening tone. "To my right is Rebecca Roberts."

Bobbs nodded.

"Nice to meet you," the host quipped. "Good looking women always serve to brighten up a busy man's day."

Meeker forced a smile as she added. "We're here on the President's behalf and at his request."

"I'm a great admirer of Mr. Roosevelt," Schmeidler chimed in. "I've voted for him three times and met him once. In my mind, he's a giant." The industrialist let his eyes drift over to a far wall. Meeker's gaze followed and noted a framed photograph of FDR hanging there. As they both studied the black and white image, Schmeidler sadly noted, "I don't have the President's courage or fortitude. To me, fear is real and it haunts me each day."

"Really?" Bobbs chimed in.

"It might sound strange," Schmeidler admitted. "I mean I'm worth millions, have thousands of employees, and pretty much am living the American dream. And yet I feel pretty powerless. I have nightmares where I lose it all. Maybe that's because I had nothing during my youth and was dirt poor when I arrived at Ellis Island. At times, I can't believe this is really my life."

"You have been blessed," Meeker noted. She then added a subtle dig. "This country's been very good to you."

He nodded. "It has. Still, even though it makes no sense, I worry I'll lose it all. People like me aren't supposed to be successful."

"Why's that?" Bobbs asked.

"Look at me," Schmeidler suggested. "I'm a little man who is afraid that at any moment everything I have will be taken from me and I won't be able to do anything about it." He paused and glanced back to the women, "But the President seems to have no fears. That's why I want to do anything I can to help him. Perhaps some of his courage and faith will rub off on me."

"We know you have supported the President," Meeker jumped in. She then qualified her praise with a second observation. "At least we know you were an early part of the lend-lease campaign. But that's not why we're here."

"Then what can I do for you?" he asked. "Do I need to add another shift at one of our plants to perhaps produce something else for the war effort? If that's what's needed, I will do it. I don't even care if there is any profit in it."

Meeker's reply was suddenly cold and biting. "Not at this time." As she looked into the man's eyes, she sensed his nervousness and decided to use it to her advantage. "You don't look like you've been sleeping very well."

He nodded. "I've been burning the candle at both ends for a long time. Several of my top men have left for the service. I'm doing about three jobs now. I just can't seem to find any good help. So, yes, I'm probably working too hard."

Meeker looked to Bobbs and nodded. Understanding the signal, the blonde jumped in and began to reveal the real reason for their visit.

"Mr. Schmeidler, I note that you have plants in Muncie, Des Moines, Chattanooga, and Tulsa."

"Among other places," he admitted. "We are mainly located in the Midwest and South though I have goals of expanding to both coasts down the road."

Bobbs continued. "The plant in Iowa, what does it produce?"

"Right now a lot of sinks and bathroom supplies," came the quick response. "They need them at our various bases here and overseas. Before the war, that plant produced the same thing except for home use."

"I believe you have a salesman in Des Moines named Newby?" Bobbs asked

"I do," he replied. "He's a good man. He would love to be serving in the military, but he has some heart issues. So that made him 4-F."

"Do you know if Mr. Newby drives a gray 1939 Chevy."

Schmeidler shook his head, "I honestly don't. About the only vehicles we buy involve our fleet of trucks."

"But," Bobbs continued, ready to spring the trap, "Even if you don't know what car was used, you are certainly aware that John Newby was the man who kidnapped a farm boy named Calvin Rawling just outside of Des Moines on June 12th."

"What?" he whispered. Finding his voice, he added, "I have no idea what you're talking about. John Newby would never be involved in something like that."

Bobbs glanced toward Meeker, who got out of her chair and moved to the window. After noting Vance and Barnes leaning up against a company truck, she turned back to their host.

"Mr. Schmeidler, your protest was much too quick and much too strong. A person who knew nothing about the crime would have first acted stunned and then stumbled a few times trying to explain Mr. Newby's innocence." She studied his eyes before delivering her next blow. "I'm going to give you one chance to come clean. If you don't, there are two men down on the street who would love the excuse to use force to pry that information out of you. Myself, I detest violence, but I loath having handicapped people kidnapped and held in order to further the cause of Nazi Germany even more." She studied the man's light blue eyes before striking her verbal knockout blow.

"There have been kidnappings in the four cities we mentioned. The men behind these crimes have been identified because of the cars they drove. It took us a while, but we traced those cars. We know those men work for you. President Roosevelt, the man who you just told us you so admire, wants those four victims back unharmed. If that happens, then we will talk about not executing you and your quartet of salesmen. So, the clock is ticking, now where are they?"

The little man weakly shook his head. "I don't what you're talking about."

Like an eagle sweeping in for the kill, Meeker hurriedly closed the distance between herself and the businessman, menacingly leaned over his desk, and pounded her fist against the wood. "The clock is ticking and I don't have time to play games. Now I don't know if the reason behind this was loyalty to the country where you were born or just a greedy man wanting more money. But no matter what it is, using innocent victims for either makes me sick to my stomach. So you need to grasp this fact … I'm onto you and the jig is up. You're going to give out the location where those four are being held even if we have to drain every drop of blood from your body." She pointed her finger toward the man's eyes before adding, "I want to make sure you understand that."

Schmeidler nodded but remained mute.

Meeker looked back to Bobbs and shrugged. She understood the signal and glanced back to her notes.

"The man behind the crime in Tulsa was Jake Cook; in Chattanooga, the person you used was Frank Taylor; and in Muncie, it was Oliver Reed. Just like Newby, all of them have worked for you for at least a decade, none has a criminal record and all have wives and children. The only reasons they are not in the military are either physical issues or age."

"You do realize," Meeker chimed in as she continued to hover over the little man, "that these men are guilty of kidnapping and the courts will show no mercy as the kidnapping was done to further the cause of a vile enemy of the United States. So not only are your wife and children going to lose a husband and father but so will those other families. Those men will go to the chair and each of those deaths will be on you."

Meeker paused and studied Schmeidler. His thin lips were drawn tight and his skin two shades lighter than it had been when they'd entered. Yet he still said nothing. Instead, he studied a framed photograph sitting on his desk. It was probably his family and the millionaire likely now understood his wife was soon to be a widow.

"Rebecca," Meeker called out, "why don't you go get the guys and let them have a piece of Mr. Schmeidler."

Bobbs nodded, pushed out of her chair, and turned toward the door. Yet before she could begin her ten-step journey, the man slowly looked away from the photo. As his eyes moved to the ceiling, Meeker sensed she had him and so she waved at Bobbs to hold her ground.

"I can't win," he whispered.

"In truth," Meeker suggested, "you'd lost before you started this game. So winning was never in the cards. We had you as soon as we put all the clues together. As a mobster recently explained to me, kidnapping is a game that leaves too many loose ends. So seasoned criminals avoid it. You should have too."

Schmeidler didn't respond but just continued to stare at his ceiling. Finally, he gave up the charade and pushed his face into his hands. He was close to cracking, but for the moment he remained mute. So, though she didn't want to, Meeker was going to have to push a bit harder to get him to spill the reason behind why an American millionaire would risk everything for the Nazis.

Walking behind the desk, Meeker pulled Schmeidler's head away from his fingers and jerked his face toward hers. Squeezing his cheeks, she hit him with one final verbal jab. "Was this about money or Nazi loyalty?"

"Neither," he whispered.

As Meeker pulled her hands back to her side, the man's head dropped until his chin hit his chest. If it wasn't about either of those, then what was the driving factor behind this crime?

"What happens to my employees?" he quietly asked still not making eye contact with either of his guests.

"You mean," Meeker cut in, "if you admit being behind this, we get the victims back, and they're healthy?"

"Yes," he whispered.

"Why did you do it?" she demanded. "I need to know that before I can even think about cutting deals."

His response came from left field. "Do you have a sister?"

"Yes, but what does that have to do with anything?"

He grimly smiled, pushed out of his chair, and walked over to a bookshelf. After retrieving a black and white, framed photo, he strolled back across the room and handed it to Meeker. As she studied an image of two smiling women, he explained.

"That's my sister and mother. They're still in Germany. Hitler has them. If I didn't grab those three girls and that boy, he was going to have Lottie and Mom killed. Only four people besides me knew about this. Those men are like brothers to me. They hate the Nazi government, but they loved me enough to kidnap those people. Believe me, each of those crippled kids is being well taken of. We would not harm them. I couldn't harm anyone."

Meeker looked to Bobbs and then back to Schmeidler. Suddenly everything was beginning to make sense.

"So," Meeker noted, "your friends were just loyal to you. They did what they did knowing that the victims would not be hurt and also knowing that your family members in Germany were pawns."

"Yes," he quietly announced as he sat back down behind his desk. "I told my four men everything. They did this for me. I want to say this again, this has nothing to do with disloyalty to the United States. They love America and so do I."

"I think," Meeker continued, "if the victims have been well

taken care of and not injured in any way, then we can protect your employees. But I to have to know where those victims are now or all bets are off."

"I can't tell you that," Schmeidler mournfully answered. "I really wish I could, but I can't. If I let you have them before the Allies and Germany make the exchange, my sister and mother will die. Would you do something that would lead to your mother's and sister's deaths?"

If only this were a matter of an immigrant being loyal to his country of birth, it would be so much easier. But his crime was convoluted beyond reason. There were no pat answers and no clear path out.

Meeker walked back toward the window and signaled for Bobbs to follow. As the two looked down toward the street, Meeker quietly stated the obvious. "Becca, we have a problem. If the kids are really safe, being well taken care of, and have not been traumatized, then shouldn't our main concern be for Schmeidler's family?"

"Helen, think about it. Schmeidler's sister's and mother's lives aren't worth two cents anyway. As soon as the Germans get wind that Armstrong is not in custody, the mother and her daughter mean nothing to Hitler. Maybe they're living now, but they're merely pawns with an execution date pending."

Meeker turned back to Schmeidler. She studied the broken man for a few moments before asking, "Who's watching the kidnapped victims?"

"My people are taking care of them," he explained, "but the locations are also being watched by Nazi agents."

"Have you met these agents?" Meeker demanded. "Are you sure they're watching?"

"No," he admitted, suddenly looking a decade older. "I was just told they were there and were recording our every move. They assured me that if we slipped up, my mother and sister would die."

"You know I'm going to check this out," Meeker warned.

"But if you're shooting straight, I can likely help you."

"I don't care about me," he announced, "but I would like my men protected."

"Okay," Meeker said, "so here's the deal. You give us the locations and we'll observe things as well."

"But Lottie and Mom," he protested, "I'm not going to sign their death warrants."

"Mr. Schmeidler," Meeker continued, "we work with an underground leader in Europe. You give us the locations so we can make sure the victims you kidnapped are all right, then we'll get our man to see if he can find and spring your mother and sister. If he does that, and as soon as we have proof they're free, we will move in and rescue the four you helped kidnap. Is it a deal?"

It was obvious Schmeidler was still skeptical. He looked back at the photograph of the two women before asking, "Can you really do that?"

"We can try," Meeker vowed. "But you have to give us what we want."

"Here's what I'll do," the industrialist meekly offered. "As soon as you can tell me where my family is and that they're alive, I'll give you the locations. But I have to have proof you have found and rescued my family first."

Meeker and Bobbs locked eyes. This was likely the best they were going to get. Now it was time to see if an underground leader they'd worked with while behind enemy lines could pull a German rabbit out of a hat.

CHAPTER II

Tuesday, June 30, 1942
7:35 p.m.
His Majesty's Royal Hospital, London, England

The flight across the English Channel was smooth and uneventful. The two German planes the Reese and Holsclaw saw completely ignored the Bf 110 Messerschmitt. Even better, the group of British de Havilland Mosquitos they met immediately noted the white boxes Reese had painted on the plane's wings and tail, did a wing salute, turned, and led the underground fighters back to a base just north of London. Once on the ground, the pair was taken immediately by ambulance to His Majesty's Royal Hospital where they were introduced to a military doctor who could have been David Niven's brother.

"You must be Reese," the physician announced as the two men strolled in through the Emergency Room door. After shaking the American's hand, the doctor turned to the other visitor. "I'm guessing that would make you Holsclaw. I'm Dr. Gene Thames. I've been looking after Mr. Strickland."

Thames was likely forty. He was a thin man whose dark hair was graying at the temples. His most distinctive features were a pencil-thin mustache and a long, narrow nose.

"Good to meet you, Doctor," Reese announced. "If you know our names, I'm assuming you know why we're here."

"Yes," he assured them. "I also know you don't have much time to waste. If you will follow me, I'll escort you to where we are treating your associate." As the white-clad Thames turned and marched down a long, well-lit hallway, he brought his guests up to speed.

"Strickland is not in the best of shape. The blast did a lot of damage. He has burns on his face and arms, some broken bones, and a lot of weakness in his legs. He's going to be our guest for a while." Stopping outside of Room 147, the doctor glanced back to Reese and Holsclaw before continuing. "In spite of his injuries, he has refused pain-killing medicines and been working from his bed. So, if you're wondering about his mind, it's as sharp as it was before the event. Still, try not to stay too long. The only way he's going to make a full recovery is if he gets a lot of rest."

"I hope won't be staying long at all," Reese assured the doctor. "We have work to do as well."

"Thanks. Now go on in and conduct your business. I'll wait outside the door."

Even though he'd been warned about the devastating nature of the injuries, Reese was nevertheless shocked. The strong, vibrant Russell Strickland he'd known was now a much different man. The right side of his face looked like raw meat, his left arm was in a cast and, from the waist down, he appeared ready to star in a horror film about a mummy. Yet, those clear, sharp and energetic eyes still shined and that crooked, likely painful smile clearly showed he was very glad to have guests.

"How are you, my friend?" Hans Holsclaw asked as the visitors approached the bed.

"Not as bad as I look," the patient assured the Dutchman. As his words were a bit slurred and his voice weak, the OSS agent's lie would have been obvious even to a blind man. Yet, even though talking caused him noticeable discomfort, Strickland charged ahead with a humorous observation. "I understand you're here to try to do my job."

"We know what Armstrong knows," Holsclaw announced with a grim nod. "Helga Smith found that out. So the job might be more important to me than you. In fact, I would say my health is now even more in doubt than yours."

Stickland's scarred face could still register shock. The OSS agent slowly shook his head before asking, "You found out why Hitler wants him? So what did I miss?"

"He knows who I am." The Dutchman emotionless answer belied the gravity of the news. "He's selling that information to the Nazis."

Strickland grimly nodded. "So you've become too much of a pain in Hitler's—"

Holsclaw cut him off. "There and other places too."

"Makes sense," Strickland noted. He paused, lost in his thoughts for a minute, before adding, "I'm guessing the news of who is leading The Shadows of Night hasn't gotten back to Germany yet."

"No," the Dutchman assured his old friend, "Armstrong is a man looking to profit; he evidently cares nothing about taking sides. When he discovered the information, he realized it had value. So he cut a deal."

"Spies who work for themselves," Strickland solemnly observed, "are the most dangerous of them all. What's he asking?"

"A box full of cash and jewels buys my name and all the other information he has gathered about my group."

"And," Reese broke into what had been a two-person exchange, "that's why we must get him now. There simply isn't time to waste. So, the question becomes, where is Armstrong?"

Strickland forced a painful shrug. "Might help if we knew how he was getting back to Germany."

"He's not," Holsclaw explained. "Helga tells us a sub is picking him up off Dover and taking him to South America. He won't give out the information until he has the ransom and is safely in a neutral country."

"He's anything but stupid," Strickland cracked with a certain degree of admiration. As his mind chewed on the new information, the bedridden agent gently rubbed his chin with his right hand and frowned. "These burns are not only painful, they itch like crazy." Once he dropped his hand back to his side, Strickland made what sounded to Reese like a morphine-inspired observation. "When you're dealing with a snake, it is best to think like one." He tapped the finger of his good hand on the bed before adding, "This snake could not have been working alone. If Armstrong found out who you and your band are then our search just widened."

"What do mean?" the Dutchman asked.

Strickland grimly smiled and explained. "Someone has loose lips in M16 or the OSS. We have to shut that person down as well." He eased his head back into the pillow and glanced toward a window. "We've had no luck finding Armstrong because we didn't know his motives or where he was headed. Now we know both. That narrows our search plan. Now, by going back to where he worked, we can see who he came into contact with on a daily basis. As only six people know your identity, Hans, we just need to uncover which of those six knew Armstrong. We should be able to ID that man pretty quickly, so the last part of this equation shouldn't take long to solve."

A now excited Reese jumped back into the discussion. "So you think Armstrong wasn't working alone."

"Now that we know what he knows," Strickland explained, "we can guess that this snake has two heads. So I'll make a few calls, uncover the other serpent and put the collar on him."

"So you think he'll talk?" Holsclaw asked.

"Not with his mouth," the OSS agent suggested, "but there are other ways people speak. You two go and get something to eat in the cafeteria. Come back in an hour or so and I'll likely have something for you … maybe a location where Nigel Armstrong is holed up."

Strickland picked up the phone from the nightstand beside his bed and Reese led the way out of the room. As they strolled out into the hall, he looked back at the Dutchman.

"Why does he think it will now be much easier to find Armstrong?"

"I have no idea," Holsclaw admitted. "I guess we'll have to have a meal, drink some coffee, and wait to find out."

CHAPTER 12

Tuesday, June 30, 1942
9:35 p.m.
His Majesty's Royal Hospital, London, England

As they entered Russell Strickland's room for the second time in two hours, the hospitalized agent seemed much more energetic. He was sitting up in bed, there were notes spread all around him, and a beautiful, brunette woman, dressed in a British army uniform, was on the phone. At any other time, Reese would have wanted to get to know this lassie much better. But sadly there was no time to waste on flirting right now; too many lives were at stake.

"Gentleman," Strickland announced, "I think I've narrowed your search grid a great deal. Pull up some chairs and listen to what Gail and I have managed to dig up."

After Reese and Holsclaw had been seated, the agent picked up the notes with his right hand and began what amounted to a briefing. His strong tone seemed to indicate he was now much closer to recovery than he'd been earlier in the evening.

"Okay. Hans, there are two men who knew your identity that also had direct and continual contact with Armstrong. At this point, I have no idea which one is working against us. And, rather than give away the fact we're onto them, I've decided to play this thing in a different way."

"How's that?" an impatient Reese demanded.

"Just hold your horses, Henry," Strickland shot back. "I think Gail just found out the key to solving this puzzle."

As the two visitors watched, the woman handed a note to the agent. He momentarily studied it before addressing his aide. "Gail, you get back to headquarters and obtain new civilian clothing and a weapon or two for Reese. Grab the rest of the stuff we talked about as well. Then bring it all back here."

Silently the woman picked up her purse and hurried out the door. Strickland didn't continue the briefing until the door was closed and the three men were again alone.

"She's my right hand," the agent explained. Then, after noting the cast on his left arm, smiled and added, "Let's make that my left hand."

"So," an impatient Holsclaw cut in, "what do you have?"

Strickland smiled and lifted his injured left arm. "You both need to sign my cast before you leave."

"Russell!" Reese barked. "Get on with it."

"Henry, you can't go anywhere until she gets back, so just hold your horses."

"Sorry."

"I accept that apology and I'll move on," Strickland said. "Now, while you were gone, I've gathered information I think will lead us to Armstrong. I've also found out something else about this case." He looked toward Holsclaw. "Hans, the new information I have is going to have to be addressed by the underground. I will fill you in on that in a second. First, as Henry is so impatient, let's begin with Armstrong.

"The only two people who could have given him the information are Warren Gibson or Phillip Yorkshire. Rather than let either one know we are onto them, I opted not to have them questioned, but instead I dug into their files to see what they revealed."

"And?" the Dutchman asked.

"And both of them own homes near Dover," Strickland explained. "I figure Armstrong must be hiding in one of those two houses or at least on one of the properties. Henry, I don't know if we have any moles in our organization, so rather than send a unit to capture Armstrong, I'm going to send you to those locations to hopefully apprehend the devil."

"Well," Reese cracked, "let's get started."

"Not yet," the agent chimed in. "Gail needs to gather the material you'll need and that will take an hour or so. Besides, I need to fill Hans in on what else I just found out and why we have to now have the underground involved. In fact, the underground is the key to solving this weird puzzle in place."

"How's that?" the Dutchman asked.

Strickland once again studied his notes. Though it seemed longer, it was likely only a bit more than a minute before the agent finally brought the visitors into his confidence.

"Thanks to Helen Meeker," Strickland explained, "as well as her team, we now know who was behind the kidnappings in the United States. It was an American industrialist named Harold Schmeidler."

"One of America's richest men is in league with Hitler?" Reese demanded.

"You know him?" the agent asked.

"I met him once when I was working for the FBI. He didn't hit me as a traitor."

"He's not," Strickland assured Reese. "He was placed in a position where he felt he had to do the Gestapo's bidding."

"I don't get it," Reese said. "How can an American be forced to turn on his own country? The German web doesn't run that far."

"It didn't have to," Strickland noted. "Schmeidler's sister and mother were still in Berlin. The Nazis now have them in custody in an unknown location. So, as can be expected, the man's love of family trumped his loyalty to country. Essentially, the fear that Hitler would kill his loved ones caused him to help nab the four polio victims."

"Okay," Reese noted. "I can buy that."

The OSS agent frowned. "I can understand that too, but here is the real issue. Schmeidler's not giving up the kidnapped kids unless we rescue his mother and sister and get them safely to England."

"Wow," Reese announced with the shake of a head, "as the English say, this is a very sticky wicket. How do we crack this nut?"

"Though the underground," Strickland answered. Turning his eyes from the American to the Dutchman, he asked, "Is there a way we can find out where the Gestapo is holding the two women?"

"Helga could likely get that information," the Dutchman quickly replied. "But even with a location, rescuing them would not be easy. The Germans likely have them well-guarded."

"Let's worry about the location first," Strickland suggested, "Then we'll figure out the next step. How can you get the information to Helga so she can start working her magic?"

Holsclaw grimly smiled. "To do that, I must drop out of this mission. You see, I must see Helga in person. The other method of contacting her, which is through ads in Berlin newspapers, would take must too long. Can you arrange to have me dropped outside Berlin?"

"When you can leave?" the OSS agent asked.

"Early tomorrow morning. I'll need to get a few things for this operation. How much time do we have?"

"Not much," Strickland soberly explained. "The woman and her daughter will only be safe until the Nazis get the information from Armstrong or until the hostages in America are found. So you likely have no more than a couple of days. I can get you all the background we have on the women. We've secured a few photos as well. You can study them on the trip back across the pond."

"So I guess I'll be working alone?" Reese asked.

"No," Strickland assured the American, "Gail will be going with you. She knows the area and if she runs into either Gibson or Yorkshire, she has a cover that will keep the guilty party from realizing we are onto him. And don't worry about Gail, she's a crack shot and her instincts are better than anyone's in this room. And that's saying a great deal."

Strickland paused before looking toward Holsclaw. "This is not going to be an easy job. It will put you and Helga in grave danger."

"We're used to it," the Dutchman solemnly assured his old friend.

"Yeah," Strickland noted, "besides uncovering the location for the women, see if Helga can find out if the Nazis were working blind with Armstrong. If they don't know what he looks like, then we might work that to our advantage as well."

"Will do," Holsclaw answered.

"Well," the injured agent announced, "now we have to wait on Gail. Would either of you like to play a few hands of poker?"

CHAPTER 13

Wednesday, July 1, 1942
6:35 a.m.
Two miles outside Dover, England

Henry Reese glanced over at the uniformed woman behind the wheel of the American-built Ford sedan. Sergeant Gail Worel stood just a bit more than five-five, she likely tipped the scales on the south side of one-fifteen and her dark brunette hair was styled to fit under her Women's Auxiliary Air Force hat. Freckles dotted her fair skin and her brown eyes sparkled in the morning sunlight. Still, as she held her back ramrod straight and wore an expression to match, even if she did look a bit like Vivian Leigh, Reese was not tempted to flirt with the Englishwoman.

"The house is just over that hill," she sternly announced as she pulled the Ford into a meadow. "I recommend we walk from here. No reason to announce our arrival or our intentions."

Reese, dressed in a gray suit, pulled his gun from where it lay on the car's bench seat and opened the door. The air felt crisp and clean and he could smell the unseen ocean via a light breeze. If he hadn't just noted the damage in Dover wrought by German bombs, he could have almost conned himself into believing there was no war raging across the globe. But, there were signs of destruction all around him as well as fresh graves in the cemetery, so there was no escaping the horrors of the worldwide conflict. This small operation was a part of it too. Thus, there was a chance soon more fresh blood would be spilled on the English soil.

"Mr. Reese," Worel announced in a crisp, proper tone, "as we found nothing at Gibson's home, I would suggest that our man is likely somewhere on Yorkshire's estate."

"Call me Henry," the American suggested.

"I see," came the quick reply. "You weren't by any chance named after a British king were you?"

"No," he admitted. "I was named after a grandfather. The closest he came to royalty was smoking Prince Albert Tobacco."

"So you're a commoner."

"And proud of it," he bragged. "Now what do I need to know about the estate?"

"Not much," Worel explained. "Though the soil is rocky and the trees small, thanks to the green, lush pasture land, the estate is postcard beautiful this time of the year. On the property, the main home has a dozen or so rooms; there are also two barns, one large and one small, a carriage house and a tiny building hiding the well and a pump. As Yorkshire only uses the home as a weekend retreat, there should be no one here."

"No servants?" Reese asked.

"No," she assured him, "they only come up when the master is present."

As they topped the hill, the American studied the scene. He could see the blue waters of the channel beyond at the base of a meadow. At a different time, it would have been a beautiful place to sit and watch the waves, but, for the moment, the view was secondary as he had far more important things to study. The property's buildings were constructed of stone with the wood trim dark green. Ivy covered the north wall of the two-story house. An apple tree stood in the front yard, but otherwise there were no trees or hedges within a hundred yards of the home. So there was no way to get to the house without being noticed.

"How old is this place," he asked.

"The house was likely built when you were still paying taxes to the crown," she quipped.

"As we obviously can't sneak up on the place," the American noted, "What do you suggest?"

"You Yanks are always wanting to sneak," Worel noted. "Is that built into your blood or something? I mean why do you think like that?"

"Because we don't like being shot," he suggested.

"Well," she cracked, "if you jolly well want to sneak up on that house I propose you go back to town and get a shovel. As tough as this dirt is, you still might be able to dig a tunnel in ten years or so."

"Was that necessary?" he asked.

"You're in England," she noted. "Let's do this the English way."

"Miss Worel, I want to still be breathing when this day is over."

"Sergeant," she corrected him. "Miss is for civilians."

"So, Sergeant, what's your plan?"

"Keep your gun ready and in your coat pocket," she explained. "If Armstrong is there and makes a move, don't bother talking it out. Just blow a hole right through the pocket."

"What if he shoots us first?" Reese demanded.

"He won't," she coolly replied. "He doesn't want anyone to know he's there. I mean if that nosy mailman hadn't noted a figure in a window yesterday, he'd still be invisible."

"Okay, that makes sense," the man admitted. "But as we are pretty sure the person in the house is Armstrong, might I ask a wee bit of a question."

"Certainly."

"Have you ever shot anyone?"

A bit of Worel's British reserve melted. Flashing a grin she quipped, "I'll take you by their graves later. Now, as far as a plan,

I'm going to go down and knock on the front door. You move around to the back and cover the rear. If Armstrong walks out your way, I'd suggest you try to shoot his kneecaps. Strickland would like him alive. How does that sound?"

"Fine. Let's get moving. But so help me, if he shoots us on our way to the house, you will never hear the end of it."

She smiled, that cool, proper British smile and moved forward. Carefully searching for any movement, he followed her step by step until the front walk. At that point, he veered to the left and circled the home. Nearing the back door, he heard the strains of a BBC newscast filtering through an open window. It appeared someone was home. As there was nothing to do know but wait, the American opted to listen to the news.

In North Africa, the British 8th Army, helped by the Allied air forces, beat back an attack by the Desert Fox, General Rommel, and drove the Nazi tank corps back more than two miles. Meanwhile, in Russia, Stalin is attempting to rally his troops as the Soviet Army retreated toward Moscow under a withering Nazi attack.

In weather, cooler temperatures are expected by mid-week with chances of rain on both Thursday and Friday. Though no rain is expected tonight, clouds will likely cover an almost full moon during the evenings.

Now, let's return to music this hour featuring pop songs by American artists.

As the Andrews Sisters singing "Don't Sit under the Apple Tree with Anyone Else but Me," by the Harry James Orchestra filled the air, Reese eased against the stone wall and looked toward the water. It was, as Worel had described it, postcard beautiful. There was a clean, fresh taste to the air and the morning sun reminded the man of a time years ago when he spent a week camping with his family. Life was simple then, there were no cares or worries and each day offered the promise of another to follow. If it was only that way now, he might just try and convince the sergeant to sit with him under the front apple tree. Of course, as cool as she was, that would mean he'd really have to put the defrost mode in high gear. Still, he liked challenges.

Reese was awakened from that dream and the peace it brought by what had to be Worel loudly rapping on the home's front door. Yanking his gun from his coat, he turned his gaze back toward the door and waited for action.

Evidently no one responded to her initial knock because the woman soon repeated the action. When this rapping also went unanswered, she opted to deliver a vocal message. For a small woman, she had a big voice.

"Nigel Armstrong, we know you are in there and we have the house surrounded. If you want to live, come out with your hands up. If you'd rather die, we can arrange that as well. The choice is yours. You have one minute."

Rather than counting the seconds, Reese studied the longest hand on his wristwatch. He continued to carefully follow it until the time expired.

"I'm coming in," Worel announced with a booming shout. A second later he heard a shot. As it had originated outside the home, he figured the sergeant was likely shooting the door's lock. A few short seconds later creaking hinges indicated she had it open.

Playing it by ear, Reese crept up to the back entry and tried the knob. It wasn't locked. Stepping to one side, he eased the door open. Just as he did, three shots rang out.

Moving quickly into what was the kitchen, the American glanced both directions. Seeing no one in a small study or the dining room, he quickly crept to another door. Just as he placed his left hand in position to swing it open, four more shots were fired.

There was no time to waste now. Taking a deep breath, he tossed the door open just in time to see a man taking aim at Worel. The woman, fully aware of the situation, lifted her right arm and squeezed the trigger. Her gun must have jammed as nothing happened.

As Worel quickly examined her weapon, the man who had to be Armstrong paused and grinned. That short-lived grin saved a woman's life and set a spy on a path to the guardhouse. Before the smiling Armstrong could fire, a still unnoticed Reese put his pistol to work. The American's first shot hit the fugitive in the stomach. The second entered his shoulder causing the spy's gun to fall to the ground. A now stunned Armstrong, the grin wiped from his face, fell against a wall, but somehow regained his balance enough to somehow stumble toward the front door. Remembering Worel's suggestion, Reese fired his weapon again, this time catching the spy in the right knee. After screaming, Armstrong fell to the floor.

Before approaching the wounded man, Worel retrieved his gun. Once she'd secured it, she marched over, grabbed the fugitive's coat and roughly turned him face up. As she studied the injuries, she cracked, "You should have just come out with your hands up. It would have saved you a lot of bloody pain."

"Get me a doctor," he demanded.

"I'll get to that in time," the woman announced, "but first I want to make sure you can afford his fee."

Reese stepped closer. It was obvious now to both him and likely Worel that this was Nigel Armstrong. He looked just like the photo they'd been given the night before. It was also apparent by the amount of blood the man was leaking, they were going to have to get help soon or the spy was going to expire. The woman didn't really look she cared if the guy checked out.

"Get me a doctor," Armstrong pleaded again. "I'm going to bleed to death."

"Then pay your fee in a hurry," Worel suggested.

"What do you mean?" the fugitive cried out.

"When and where is the U-boat going to pick you up?"

"What are you talking about?" Armstrong yelled. "Get me some help, I'm dying."

Worel turned toward Reese and shrugged. "Henry, we've done all we can do here. Guess we'll head back to London. Yorkshire will likely come here this weekend. Maybe he can help the bloke."

As a shocked Armstrong looked on, Reese followed the WAFF sergeant into the living room. She was just reaching for the doorknob when the wounded man screamed, "Monday at midnight."

Worel didn't bother returning to the parlor where the man lay. She used her huge voice to shout out, "Where?"

"Two miles north of the cliffs. I'm supposed to row out a mile and wait for them to surface."

The woman looked at Reese and smiled. Yet, rather than return to Armstrong, she barked out another long-range question.

"Armstrong, how long has Yorkshire been working with the Nazis?"

"He's not," came the pained response. "I stole the information the Nazis wanted from his safe. You see, I know the code. He has no idea I'm here."

"Are you on the up and up?" Worel demanded.

"Yes."

Strolling over to a desk, she picked up the phone's receiver, twisted a crank and waited. A few seconds later she said, "This is Sergeant Gail Worel of the WAFF. I need a doctor to come immediately to the Yorkshire Estate; a man has been shot." After slipping the receiver back into the base, she casually looked at Armstrong. "I guess we need to see if we can slow down the bleeding. Why don't you get some towels out of the bathroom and I'll play nurse."

Reese shook his head. She was one tough cookie. He now doubted if she'd ever join him under an apple tree, but if they ever allowed women in combat, he'd want her in his unit.

CHAPTER 14

Thursday, July 2, 1942
8:22 p.m.
A country estate outside of Stendal, Germany

The small city of Stendal was almost a thousand years old. Located north of Berlin, the German hamlet was best known for Tangermuder Tor, a brick tower featuring a gate opening into the heart of the community's business district. Unlike many German cities, Stendal had so far escaped the fierce Allied bombings, but that didn't mean the war had not touched its people. Almost everyone in Stendal had lost a son or husband and with each passing day, the list of those who'd given their lives for the Fatherland grew longer.

On a small, country estate just outside the city, Hans Holsclaw and six men were hidden in a grove of trees. Dressed as Nazi soldiers, they were studying the eight-room stone house that had once belonged to a prominent Lutheran pastor. In 1939, the Gestapo made the preacher an offer he couldn't refuse and, after selling for only a small portion of its actual value, the property became a retreat for some of Hitler's top dogs. Yet, the home that usually hosted parties was now serving as a jail for two women who once thought they'd escape the war. Now they found themselves pawns in a game that likely had no happy ending.

Lottie Schmeidler was thirty-two, blonde, blue-eyed, and plain. She was serving as a librarian in Berlin when the Gestapo picked her up. Gretchen Schmeidler, in her late sixties, was a heavy-set lady with large hazel eyes and gray hair. The Nazis nabbed her from her apartment. After answering routine questions about their family, the women were then transported by truck to the estate and locked in an upper bedroom. Though unharmed, they understood their ultimate fates rested in the hands of Gretchen's son in St. Louis. If he didn't give in to the Nazis' demands, the women would be shot.

Thanks to information provided by Helga Smith, Holsclaw learned the guard was changed at eight-thirty each evening. At that time, a trio that worked the night shift replaced three Gestapo men serving as the day watch. Other than letting the women out for bathroom breaks and providing them with meals, Smith had also discovered the guards did little but listen to the radio, play cards, and swap war stories. Thus, given the element of surprise, the raid to free the hostages should not be that difficult or costly. However, once they had freed the women, transporting them across Europe and to London would be a major challenge.

"There's the truck," Fitz Banner whispered.

Holsclaw looked down the dusty road, nodded, and calmly observed the German military vehicle pull into the driveway. Three men dressed in civilian clothes exited, strolled down the walk and, after knocking, used a key and opened the front door. Less than a minute later, the trio that had been inside exited the home, ambled back to the truck, got in, put the vehicle into reverse, pulled out onto the road, and headed toward Stendal. The exchange was now complete.

"Is it time?" an anxious Fitz asked.

"Yes," the leader acknowledged. He looked back to his team. "Okay, we've rehearsed this a dozen times. Fitz, Willie, and Wolf go with me to the front door. As we explain that we've had car trouble, the three of you burst in the back door. Don't wait for them to draw their guns, just shoot them down where they stand."

Holsclaw glanced back toward the house and continued, "I don't know if the gunfire will draw any attention from town or not, but let's assume it will. That means we have between three and five minutes to get the women and get them back to our truck. If there is any delay, it might mean a battle and we'd likely be outnumbered. So don't waste time and don't show any mercy. As soon you three move around to the back of the home, we'll go knock on the front door. When you sense we have the guards' full attention, charge in."

The trio quickly dispersed and made their way around the stone home. When they were out of sight, Holsclaw and his group stepped out into the road and walked down the drive to the front door. Maintaining a casual mood, they kept their side arms in the holsters. With a steady hand, the Dutchman rapped on the wooden entry. A few moments later a voice called out from the inside.

"State your name and business."

"Major Hans Bloom, our truck had a flat about a half mile down the road. Some idiot didn't replace the jack and I need to borrow one to change it."

The door cracked open. A man holding an automatic studied the visitors before swinging the entry far enough to allow the men to enter. The Gestapo officer's gun followed Holsclaw as the Dutchman walked into the room. The other two guards stood in the living room with their rifles ready as well.

"Why all the firepower?" Holsclaw asked. "Are we Germans now fighting each other as well as the Allies?"

"We are with the secret police," the one with the Lugar announced, "and there as been a lot of underground activity in this area. We need to make sure you are who you appear to be."

"You can trust us," the Dutchman assured them.

"We trust no one," came the quick reply.

97

Holsclaw smiled. "That's hardly a good way to go through life."

A split-second later the backdoor burst open and the fireworks began. The clean operation Holsclaw had envisioned didn't play out as planned. While one of the Gestapo guards was immediately hit and killed, the other two manage to squeeze off several rounds before the underground's bullets found them. Counting the three members of the secret police, the home was now playing host to five dead men.

The Dutchman wanted to curse, but he didn't have the time. Even though he'd lost two, the team still had an objective to meet.

"If our information is correct," he barked, "the women are up those stairs and to the right. Fritz, you and Frank check it out."

The men had only climbed two of the eleven steps when the sound of vehicles could be heard through the still open front door. Rushing over to the window, Holsclaw got a feel for their quickly changing landscape.

"At least a dozen soldiers," he yelled. "They're jumping out of a truck and fanning out all around us. There are some more folks getting out of two staff cars."

"What do we do?" Fritz asked.

Holsclaw shook his head. They were outnumbered, outgunned, and surrounded. Glancing back to his four remaining men, the Dutchman asked, "Have any of you ever read about a battle in America called the Alamo?"

They all shook their heads. Their leader smiled; maybe it was better they weren't students of history. Sometimes knowing the last few pages can really ruin a story.

"Two of you cover the back," Holsclaw suggested, "the rest stay here. We'll hold them off as long as we can. Perhaps we can do enough damage to rush out of the house and make a dash for home."

As they got in position, a voice called. It appeared that the

Gestapo was about to offer a deal. If that were the case, it would be the first time.

"You men inside. Give up now and we won't kill you. And, we won't kill the two women you likely came to rescue. But if you don't throw out your weapons and appear in the next minute, you will all die."

"We fight?" Fritz more demanded than asked.

"No," Holsclaw bluntly replied.

"But ..."

The Dutchman cut him off. "We have no chance if we stay here and fight. But, we at least have a chance to escape if they capture us. We go with the odds." Moving back to the door, Holsclaw yelled, "We will throw down our weapons and come out with our hands up." He turned back to his men. "Toss your guns out the door."

"Are you sure about this," Fritz questioned.

"No," Holsclaw admitted, "but the odds are better for us living to fight another day if we give up now."

After all the weapons had been tossed out the open door, the Dutchman called out, "That's everything, including the weapons of your dead comrades. Are you going to keep your word and not kill us?"

"You are too valuable to kill," came the cold reply.

Holsclaw looked back to his quartet. "We are not giving up, we are just buying time. When we have the right numbers, we will make a break. Now let's act like we're going along with them."

The Dutchman led his men out the front door. With their hands over their heads, they marched silently down the drive to the road. A balding, slightly overweight man wearing a dark suit met them.

"You were wise to give up," he said with a sly smile.

"We had no real choice," Holsclaw replied.

An enlisted man emerged from the shadows. "Do you want my men to take them back to town?"

"No," came the order, "you gather your troops, get back into that truck and leave. My six men will be more than enough to handle this crew. After I visit with their leader for a while, we'll load them into our truck and take them back to Berlin."

As Holsclaw watched, the dozen regular soldiers assembled in front of the house got into the truck and, within two minutes of the order, they were headed to town. During that time, six dark-clad members of the secret police, each armed with a rifle, took a position about a half dozen feet right of the Dutchman and his men. Things still looked bleak, but at least the odds were now more in their favor.

"Your name?" the leader asked as he pulled a cigarette from his pocket and lit it.

"Major Hans Bloom," Holsclaw replied.

"I know better than that," came the quick reply. "You're leader of The Shadows of Night."

"What is that?" The Dutchman asked. "It sounds like one of those American cowboy bands."

Their captor laughed. "Don't play me for a fool. I'm Roderick Adelmann and my boss is Himmler. And when I was told that you would raid this home tonight, I was prepared. Hitler will likely give me a medal for bringing you down. There is also a nice reward that I will be happy to spend."

"I suggest," Holsclaw quipped, "you get that reward in British pounds, I'm not betting on the German mark having much value when this little circus closes."

"You won't be so funny when we get you in front of a firing squad."

The sound of a door opening drew both men's attention back to a Mercedes staff car. Exiting from the back seat was an elegantly dressed woman. She held a coat over her right arm and moved down the road with the grace of a dancer.

"Helga," Adelmann announced, "your information was correct."

Smith stepped up closer to Holsclaw and smiled. "Roderick,

this man is the head of the underground unit that's been terrorizing the Fatherland."

Holsclaw shook his head in disbelief. A woman he'd trusted and even felt sorry for had played him. She'd strung him along until he'd ended up hanging himself. But why had she waited for so long? Why hadn't she ratted him out a year ago?

CHAPTER 15

Thursday, July 2, 1942
9:02 p.m.
A country estate outside of Stendal, Germany

Hans Holsclaw was in shock. It seemed the entire time Helga Smith was feeding him information, she was also setting him up. Glancing to his left he watched the Gestapo guards, their guns at their sides, taking in the unexpected drama playing out on the country estate. The very woman who'd come up with this plan, given them the location, and assured them everything would come off without a hitch was now standing just ten feet in front of the Dutchman with a placid, frigid smile framing her beautiful face. Now he wished he had chosen to emulate the men who were at the Alamo.

"What is your real name?" Adelmann demanded.

"I'll never tell you," Holsclaw answered.

"It's Hans Holsclaw," Smith chimed in. "He's a cobbler in Amsterdam. I can give you his address. He has a family; you can pick them up and take them off to the camps. They'll make good slave labor for our war effort."

"Holsclaw," Adelmann whispered, letting the name all but drip off his tongue. "The Fuhrer will love this."

"But," Smith noted, "He'll have to find out on his own."

"What do you mean?" Adelmann demanded.

"Because," the woman announced with a sly smile, "this is where the train ride ends."

As a confused Adelmann watched, Smith dropped her coat to the ground and aimed the machine gun she'd hidden under it in both hands. In less than a blink of an eye, the night was filled with noise. Before the stunned Gestapo troops could even fire their weapons, the woman had mowed them down. As the black uniformed soldiers fell to the ground, she turned back to the man who had been her lover.

"Wait!" he demanded.

"As I said," she announced, "the train ride ends here."

"Do you know what you just did?" Adelmann demanded.

"And I'm not through," she taunted.

"But I gave you everything," he barked.

"What you really gave me was enough information to sink a few battleships. You were my source."

"But ..."

"Think about that," she coldly announced, "I used you; you didn't use me." As the woman's betrayal slowly sank in, Smith offered one more bit of advice. "You should have never cheated on your wife. There are always consequences." She then pulled the trigger again. Four shots rang out and a still stunned Adelmann fell to the ground.

"We need to hurry," the seemingly satisfied woman announced as she handed the weapon to Holsclaw.

"What's this all about?" the Dutchman asked.

"The door to the women's room is booby-trapped. If it had been forced open, you and the captives would have been blown to kingdom come. That was the one detail I found out too late to warn you, so I had to try to save you this way."

As Holsclaw's men grabbed firearms, Smith looked toward the house. "On the top of the door of the room where the women are being held there's a pin. Pull it up and it disconnects the bomb."

"Did you hear that, Fritz?" the Dutchman called out.

"Yes, sir. We will go get them."

As the quartet hurried into the house to rescue the two members of Harold Schmeilder's family, Holsclaw turned back to Smith. "I guess you'll have to come with us. I think there's room to get you to London."

The woman solemnly nodded. "I need a vacation. I still have some relatives outside of Cardiff, maybe I can stay with them for a while."

The Dutchman turned back toward the house and yelled, "Come on. We need to get moving."

Hearing a click behind him, Holsclaw turned just in time to see Smith's face go ashen white. A single gunshot rang out and the woman doubled over at the waist. A gun in his hand, the man he thought was dead had managed to rise to one knee. A single blast from the Dutchman's machine gun put the Gestapo man back on the ground. This time there would be no getting up. After kicking Adelmann to make sure he was down for the count, Holsclaw hurried over to the wobbly Smith's side. She collapsed into his arms just as he arrived.

"Guess you can cancel my reservation," she whispered.

He didn't have time to reply before the woman went limp. Easing Smith to the ground, he went down on one knee and hesitantly checked her pulse. There was none.

"We have them," Fritz announced as he led the two women through the home's front door.

"Move them quickly to our truck," the Dutchman ordered.

"Are you coming, sir?" one of the men asked as they rushed by.

"I will be along," he assured them.

As the underground men disappeared into the field across the road, Holsclaw moved his hand over the beautiful woman's face. Now it was up to God to judge if what the preacher's kid had done for the war effort was too great a sin for her to be admitted to Heaven. After closing her eyes, the Dutchman rose and jogged into the shadows.

CHAPTER 16

Friday, July 3, 1942
3:31 p.m.
Harold Industrial Headquarters, St. Louis, Missouri

Sensing this was going to be a day of action, Helen Meeker had worn slacks, a pullover summer sweater, and flats. She'd forgone a hat and pulled her hair back into a ponytail. Within twenty-four hours, she hoped to have four missing people back with their families. That would indeed make this an Independence Day to remember.

The woman stood by the window in Harold Schmeidler's office and anxiously watched the industrialist on the phone. Outside, her three team members were waiting by Capone's old green Cadillac with rescue on their minds. Each of them had an assignment and was ready to spring into action, but nothing could or would happen until this bridge was crossed. Schmeidler had to be convinced that Meeker had fulfilled her part of the bargain.

The look on the industrialist's face when she'd walked in proved he was hopeful, yet when she'd given him the news that his sister and mother were in London he surprisingly didn't show much excitement. Then, when he accused her of playing him, she almost lost her cool and slapped him. Even when she presented the man with a wire photo of the two women pictured with the Union Jack behind them, he wasn't ready to provide the information Meeker so badly wanted. Thus, she had to waste even more time setting up an overseas phone call. That had changed this whole exercise from a short meeting into a marathon bartering session. It took a full hour just to get the call through finally.

As soon as he heard a voice on the other end, Schmeidler's mood changed. As he was naturally speaking in German, Meeker had very little idea as to what he was saying, but at least his face indicated he finally realized the impossible had been accomplished and the women were safe. When he ended the short call and set the receiver back into the phone's cradle, tears filled his eyes.

"Amazing," he whispered. "I didn't think it was possible."

Remaining by the window, Meeker folder her arms and pushed toward her own objective. This time she was not going to be put off.

"Now we need the addresses."

The industrialist nodded, walked over to the bookshelf, pulled out a well-worn Bible and, with the woman peering over his shoulder, began to leaf through the pages. It was somewhere in the book of John he found what he was searching for.

"Here you go," he announced as he held up the paper.

Meeker quickly took the notecard and studied the four addresses. The victims were being held in different locations. The Rawling kid was in Rockford, Illinois; Andrew Reason was being held in Nashville; Madge Crawford was in Gary, Indiana; and Amy Boatright was in Denton, Texas.

"As you can see," Schmeidler announced, "they're all in motor courts. It was easiest that way. I could hide them and keep them comfortable. Besides, I could rent them by the week and they were fairly low traffic areas. Places like that gave us more privacy than hotels."

Meeker nodded as she slipped the paper into her pocket. "You need to call those men holding each of these people and let them know law officials will be coming to pick them up. Do you understand?"

"I will do that," he agreed. "I always go to a payphone once a day and check on them. I guess now that I'm not worried about having the line tapped, I can use this phone." He paused, took a deep breath and turned his eyes to the wire photo Meeker had given him. After studying the picture for a moment, he said, "Thank you for getting them back."

Her answer, given in a measured tone, was not sympathetic. "There was a price. The woman who uncovered where your mother and sister were being held is dead. So are two members of the underground who took part in the rescue operations."

Schmeidler shook his head. "I'm sorry."

"You should be," she angrily snapped.

The smile now wiped from his face, he quietly asked, "I guess you're going to arrest me for what I did as well?"

Meeker shrugged. "I don't know what the government will do to you; my concern is for those four people who you grabbed. I want to see them back home safely with their families. But even if the government doesn't do anything, I want you to always remember that three lives were sacrificed for your family." She moved toward the door, grabbed the knob, and pulled it open. She paused for a moment then turned back to the man.

"Schmeidler, those two members of the underground left their wives and six children behind. I hope your family was worth that sacrifice."

Meeker didn't wait for the man's reply. Nothing he said would have satisfied her anyway.

CHAPTER 17

Friday, July 3, 1942
7:35 p.m.
Water's Edge Motor Court and Lodge
outside of Nashville, Tennessee

The rain was pouring as Becca Bobbs navigated the two-lane mud road outside of Nashville, Tennessee. She was headed to a small motor court located on Crippled Creek, a tributary of the Cumberland River. The facility was mainly used by sportsman for either hunting or fishing exhibitions, but, in a huge departure from the norm, Harold Schmeidler opted to stash a crippled child in one of the Water's Edge cabins. Now it rested with Bobbs to pick up Andrew Reason and take him back to his mother.

After flying into the Tennessee capitol, Bobbs rented a 1939 Nash and then made a call to Washington D.C. Alison Meeker provided a quick update on the rest of the team. Helen had easily found Calvin Rawling and was now driving the boy back to his father in Iowa. Vance was still enroute to rescue Madge Crawford and strangely, in the only rescue that seemed to be taking a wrong turn, Barnes had not been able to locate Amy Boatright. With that news in hand, Bobbs drove through a deluge toward the lodge hoping her job would go smoothly as had Meeker's.

The motor court's main building was located on a hill overlooking the now rushing Crippled Creek. Bobbs hurried from the car to the covered porch and, before entering, studied the dozen log cabins dotting the hillside. The rushing water was licking two and, if the rains didn't stop, three more would soon be in danger of flooding. Even the ducks were likely seeking cover today.

Pushing open the door into the combination bait shop-grocery on a mission, she hurried by a Coke machine, a candy display, and a shelf lined with artificial bait and colorful lures. Her objective seemed to not care a wit about the weather as he sat on a stool behind a counter, holding a knife in one hand and a hunk of hickory in other. She guessed the white-headed, wisp of a man with steel blue eyes and heavily wrinkled skin was whittling a child's toy. On a different day, she would have asked about it, but at this moment she had no time for small talk.

"Can I help you?" his voice was high and displayed a strong southern drawl.

"I'm looking for a boy?"

"Did you lose one?" he joked.

She shook her head. "I'm here to pick him up. He's crippled."

"Oh," the old man said with a nod, "that kid. He's staying in Cabin 1. I guess that his uncle is with him. At least that what I was told when they rented that place a few weeks back."

"So they're still here?" Bobbs asked.

"Well, they were," he explained, "but now that I think about it, the uncle pulled out about an hour ago. I don't remember seeing the kid in the car when he left. I guess he went to get some food or something. He's done that a few times over the last few weeks and he always leaves the boy behind."

"Which cabin is he in?" Bobbs ask.

The old man put the knife and wood on the counter and eased off the stool. He stretched and complained, "My old bones don't like all this rain." After rubbing his lower back, with a noticeable limp, he moved out from behind the counter, around Bobbs and headed toward the door. She followed him step by step until he stopped out on the porch. Peering through the rain he made a sobering observation.

"Creek's come up a lot in the past ten minutes." He then pulled his baseball hat back and scratched his head. "I wonder if the dam's letting go?"

"What dam?" the woman yelled over the rain peppering the porch's tin room.

"There's an earthen dam about five miles upstream," the man explained. "They built it to make a small lake. As much rain as we've had, the water has to be lapping over the top of the dam right now. That's why the water's so high."

Bobbs studied the raging creek. The water was rising so quickly, she could see it climbing higher up the bank each second. As she tried to get a gauge on how high the water might go, the old man made a troubling observation.

"They didn't build that dam very well, so if it's lapping over then the force of the water will soon push that thing down. When that happens, this whole valley's going to fill up with water and I'll lose half my cabins."

Bobbs glanced back to the creek. It had to be up at least two feet since she'd arrived. She had to get Andrew out now. There was no time to wait.

"Which cabin is the boy in?" she yelled.

"The one down there," he said as he pointed.

"Right by the river?"

"Yeah, and the water's already covering the porch."

Sensing the danger, Bobbs raced down the muddy hill. She only made twenty feet when she tripped on a rock and fell headfirst into the mud. Pulling herself off the ground, she looked back at the angry stream. It was rising more quickly now and she was still a hundred yards from the cabin. Splashing through red mud, she made another fifty years before the rain gave way to hail. By the time she got to the cabin, she was being struck by ice the size of golf balls.

The cabin was only about twenty by fifteen feet and constructed of logs. Its roof was metal and there was a stone chimney on the near side. There were just four small windows and only one door located in the middle of the front porch. So there was one way in and one way out and the water was already covering that route.

Wading through knee-deep water, Bobbs hung onto the porch railing to keep the current from knocking her off her feet. Catching her breath she glanced back at the creek. It was dark, muddy and filled with debris. Continuing to employ the railing for support, she pulled through the now raging water to the front door. Grabbing the knob, she tried to push it open. It wouldn't give.

Climbing up onto an old church pew positioned under one of the windows, she stepped out of the water and looked inside. Andrew Reason was there, huddled on a couch. She tapped the window attempting to get him to look her way, but the pounding hailstones likely kept him from hearing. She then tried to raise the glass, but it wouldn't budge.

Glancing back at the creek, she noted the water was continuing to climb at an alarming rate. It was now even creeping up onto the pew where she stood. She had to do something, but what? Looking to the north, she saw a four-foot-long limb headed her way. Stepping off the bench, she held onto the porch rail, leaned out and grabbed the hunk of wood with her left hand. Reeling it in, she waded back across the porch and climbed back on the pew. Grabbing the limb with both hands, she swung it like Jolting Joe DiMaggio. As wood connected with glass, the window busted into a hundred pieces. After using the limb to knock away the shards still clinging to the pane, she grabbed the top of the window framing and swung her legs through. She sat there for a moment, catching her breath, before dropping to the floor. Across the room, a small boy smiled.

Wading across the floor, she leaned over and put her arms

around Andrew Reason. Screaming to be heard over the falling hail and rolling thunder, she announced, "My name's Becca and we've got to get out of here. I'm stronger than I look. I'll carry you up that hill so we can get away from the creek. Do you understand?"

He must have figured it was much better to go with a stranger than challenge the flood. Nodding, he wrapped his arms around the woman's neck and cried out, "I'm ready."

There was no current in the house, just standing water, so it was fairly easy for Bobbs to move across the room. Sensing that navigating the porch without holding onto the rail would be impossible, she opted to head toward one of the back windows. With Reason riding her piggyback, she reached up, undid the clasp, and forced it up.

"Andrew," she yelled, "I'm going to lift you up and push you through the window. Can you hold into the cabin until I get through?"

"Yes," he screamed back. "My arms are strong."

As he loosened his grip on her neck, Bobbs turned, picked the boy up in her arms, and lifted him to the windowsill. After pushing his useless legs through, she placed her arms around his chest and lowered him to the ground. As the back of the cabin was a bit further up the hill, the water he now rested in was only about a foot deep. Wasting no time, Bobbs grabbed the window frame and swung her legs through the opening. A couple of seconds later she was also on the ground.

"Let's ride," she yelled as she stooped down beside the boy.

After he had slid his arms around her neck, she pushed upright. The current was pretty strong, but not like had been on the porch. If she could just manage twenty short steps, she'd once more be on ground that was muddy but not covered by the creek.

Bobbs had taken five steps before she heard what sounded like a thousand lions all roaring at once. Looking to her left, she found the noise's source. The dam must have given way; there was a twenty-foot high wall of water headed down the valley. Panic drove her to try to race up the hill. Likely, if she hadn't been carrying a boy, she could have made it, but today she was five steps short when the water hit.

Initially, the wave wall pushed both Bobbs and Reason under water. Surrounded by logs, brush, and even old car tires, the woman was pushed deep and trashed like clothes in an automatic washer. Bobbs thought her lungs would burst before she finally shot above the surface and grabbed a taste of air. Holding her head above the raging tide she tried to find her bearings as she was swept down the valley. Though she'd guessed she'd only been underwater for perhaps thirty seconds, it appeared she was now hundreds of yards downstream and a good fifty feet from shore in any direction. Worse yet, she didn't see the boy. Completely at the mercy of the raging water, she didn't have a chance to formulate any kind of plan before she was pushed back under the surface for the second time. When she came up again she saw a hundred foot tall, four-foot wide oak standing thirty feet ahead. There was no time to react. She hit the century-old tree hard and everything went black.

"Are you okay?" someone asked. The voice sounded like it was a hundred miles away.

Bobbs reached a muddy hand up to the top of her head and winced when she touched a bulging knot the size of a golf ball. As the fog cleared from inside her pounding skull, she became aware of the creek rushing in the background and realized it was no longer raining. Pushing her hands into what felt like a moss-covered rock, she lifted up to a sitting position to get a fix on where she was. As she peered into the night, it was far too dark to make much out.

How long had it been since she hit the tree? It seemed like seconds but, as it was now night, it must have been hours. That meant that time had essentially stopped the moment of impact.

"I thought you might die," the unidentified voice explained.

"Where am I?" Bobbs asked.

"On a creek bank somewhere. There're some lights on top of this ridge. We can likely get some help there."

The woman twisted and tried to focus. It took a few seconds, but she did finally see the lights. Based on what she was seeing, she guessed there was a house at the top of the hill. Turning with great effort, she pushed off the ground and stood. Looking down, she now actually saw the form of the figure in the darkness.

"How did I get here?" she asked. "Last thing I remember was slamming into a tree."

"I saw you were in trouble," he explained, "and I managed to get over to you and keep your head above water. We floated with the current for a while and when things slowed down, I worked my way over to the bank."

As Bobbs glanced back to the creek, a wave of sadness washed over her. She'd been just a few minutes too late to save the boy. If she hadn't stopped to call Alison at the airport, she would have probably gotten to the cabin before the water rose. If that had been the case, she'd have been taking the kid home by now. But instead, she'd let Andrew Reason down and, for the second time in a month, his mother's heart would be broken.

"You think we ought to get up to that house?" the voice asked.

Bobbs took a deep breath and nodded. "Hope they have a phone, I have some bad news I need to share. I'd like to get it over with as soon as possible."

"Sorry."

"Nothing you did," she assured him. "After all, you saved my life."

"It wasn't that big a deal," he noted. "You know it's funny, I used to be scared of the water, but now I'm a really good swimmer. You know who taught me how to swim?"

"No," Bobbs answered, not really caring.

"You may not believe it, but it was the President of the United States."

It took a moment for the words register, but as they took

root, Bobbs looked down at the figure hidden by darkness and shadows.

"Andrew Reason?" she almost yelled.

"Yeah," came the answer. "How did you know?"

CHAPTER 18

Saturday, July 4, 1942
1:45 a.m.
Eastside Motor Court, Gary, Indiana

Dizzy Vance parked his rented 1937 Dodge, opened the car's door, and moved under a large elm tree. As his eyes grew used to the light, he scoped out the scene before him. The Eastside Motor Court consisted of a dozen frame cottages positioned in a U-shape around the central office/diner. The parking lot was gravel and, as there was no lighted sign or street lamp, the only illumination came from a half-full moon. So the only way to find #5, where the kidnapped woman was waiting, was to amble through the units and look on the doors. Though he likely had nothing to fear; after all, this was supposed to be a clean pick up, he still detested being out in the open. He'd felt that way since the day his wife and son were killed.

Trying to fight off illogical fear, he rubbed his fleshy chin and attempted to analyze the best and easiest course of action. Logic dictated that the first cabin was likely the one to his left and the rest likely went in numerical order from that point. That meant the cabin he needed was at the back left corner of the business's layout. Slowly scanning the entire lot he counted six cabins that had cars parked in front of them and two of those units still displayed lights visible through the windows. The one he guessed as #5 was dark, but there was a 1941 Ford coupe parked in front. Was that where Madge Crawford was waiting?

With the logical location pinpointed, he should have moved forward, but he remained glued in place. Though he couldn't explain why, things just didn't feel right. Reaching into his pocket, his fingers went around a weapon he genuinely hoped he wouldn't have to use. Still, knowing the gun was ready and loaded brought a small sense of security, but what he really needed to bolster his strength was a stiff drink. Just one good belt would make all of this so much easier.

As the suddenly insecure investigator continued to study the dark cabin, his lips and throat grew dry. Though the night air was cool, he was also sweating bullets and his heart had found its way into his throat.

Liquid courage! That's what a friend of his once called it. With a few doses of liquid courage, any man could become Superman. The alcohol not only steadied the nerves, it gave his mind a sharper focus and it was what he needed now. If fact, he had to have it.

Spinning on his heels, Vance quickly jogged the five steps back to the Dodge, opened the door, slid in, yanked the door closed, hit the starter, and listened to the motor roar to life. Pushing in the clutch, he slipped the transmission into first and smiled. Just one shot would give him what he needed to rescue the young woman. Glancing into the rearview mirror to check if anyone was coming up the road, he noted his face barely visible in the glow of the instrument's lights.

At first Vance didn't recognize the guy staring back at him. The reflection showed a clean-shaven, clear-eyed man wearing a new fedora, white shirt, striped tie, and a blue, pinstriped suit coat. Who was he? He looked nothing the Dizzy Vance from a week before. As the investigator continued to study that unfamiliar image, it was suddenly replaced by something else.

Rather than seeing himself now, the man was being haunted by the tragic, bloated face of Mabel Grecklemeyer. In her hand, she held the bottle that he dearly wanted.

"Just one drink," she whispered, pushing the bottle his way. He jerked his eyes from the glass and looked through the windshield. She was there on the road too but now she wasn't offering him a drink, she was screaming at him. Even when he covered his ears, he could still hear her.

"You're not any better than I am and you never will be."

Closing his eyes, he tried to push the haunting image from his mind but he couldn't and she wouldn't quit screaming, her words reminding him of what he was.

"You're a drunk," she yelled. "You're nothing more than a sorry drunk."

Opening his eyes, he saw her now just hovering outside the glass. She was pushing the bottle at him and it was dripping on the windshield.

"Stop it," he screamed. "Please go away."

Looking back into the mirror, he noted his own face again. "Not going back there," he whispered.

Trembling, he took a deep breath and tried to slow his heart. Looking back over the hood he saw only the road. She was gone.

A still shaky Vance glanced back to the motor court. That's where he needed to be and taking a drink would not make the job he needed to do any easier. As a matter of fact, it would likely stop him from doing his job. Reaching down to the ignition, he switched off the key, hurriedly lifted the handle, and pushed open the door. It was time for action. Stepping back out into the cool night air, he straightened his tie and, after he managed to find some strength in his knees, began the twenty-yard march to the Eastside Motor Court's parking lot.

He'd guessed right on which unit was #5. Putting his hand on the Ford's hood, he was a bit shocked to note it was warm. That meant the car had been driven recently. Keeping his eye on the cottage's door, he stepped around the coupe and glanced inside.

121

There was nothing out of the ordinary in either of the seats, but one beat up duffle bag. Flipping on the steering column's light, he bent over to read the registration slip. The car didn't belong to Frank Taylor, the man who'd snatched Crawford for Schmeidler. So where was Taylor and who was Benny Houston?

Walking around the rear of the car, Vance pulled his gun from coat pocket and approached the door. Holding the weapon in his right hand he knocked with the left. When no one immediately answered, he knocked again, this time adding a vocal greeting.

"This is Vance. I'm here to pick up Madge Crawford."

Still no one answered.

The investigator eased his hand down and checked the knob. It turned freely. After taking a deep breath, he shoved it open and stepped inside. Reaching to his left he found a switch and turned on a single sixty watt, overhead bulb. Sitting in a chair against the far wall was Crawford. She was dressed in a light blue skirt and white blouse. She appeared shocked and frightened. To her left, spread awkwardly face down across the bed, was a well-dressed man. Two bloody holes in the back of his light blue suit coat were all the evidence Vance needed to realize that he'd died from the rapid type of lead poisoning. The investigator's attention was still locked on the victim when he noted movement to his right.

Shifting his gaze, Vance spied a partially open door likely leading to a bathroom. With all the grace he could muster, the heavyset man took four steps forward and one to the right. Pressing his back into the wall, he waited to see if the person in the bath would choose to make an entrance. As the waiting game continued and the seconds ticked by, the investigator looked back at Crawford. He expected to see her eyes locked on the bathroom, but they weren't. Instead, she was nervously staring in the direction of the open front door. Then it dawned on him. There were at least two men to worry about.

Dropping to his knee he spun toward the entry. As he did, a shot, fired from a gun equipped with a silencer, knocked the hat off his head. Realizing how close he'd come to dying, Vance fought to regain his focus and nerve. As he steadied his head, he focused on a wide-shouldered man framed in the door now readjusting his gun barrel downward. The intruder would never find out if his aim were true. Vance's shot hit the visitor right between his eyes. As the first attacker fell to the floor, the investigator whirled back toward the bath.

"I got your partner," Vance called out. "Drop your weapon and come out with your hands up or you'll be joining him."

"You want the girl?" the hidden man asked.

"Yeah. That's all I want right now, I don't need any extra baggage."

"Then you better let me walk out of here," the man warned. "You see, one of my guns is aimed straight at her head. Provide me a hall pass or she'll die."

Vance looked to Crawford. The poor woman was so frightened her hands were shaking like tree limbs in a tornado.

"Listen," the man announced. "I've got two guns. One is going to be aimed at her and the other at you. You let me walk out that door to my car and neither one of them will go off. You make a move and I'll pull both triggers at the same time."

"My gun will be on you too," Vance announced.

"So how we going to play this? Do you want all three of us to die or all three of us to walk away?"

Vance looked back to the young woman and forced a smile. Her life was all that mattered right now.

"Take a walk," Vance called out, "there's already been enough death tonight."

"Fine," came the reply, "but just don't blink or I'll fire and bring the local funeral parlor a bit more business."

Maintaining his crouching position, the investigator observed the door slowly open and the man walk out. He was about five-ten, his complexion ruddy and hair blonde. He wore a gray suit and no tie. As he moved, he kept his dark, brown eyes locked onto Vance as his guns moved just enough to keep both the investigator and the kidnapped girl in his sights.

As the man continued his slow exit, Vane made a deeper study of his opponent's face so that he would know him if they ever met again. Then, like a bolt from the blue, it hit him. The gunman somehow looked familiar. Somewhere, at some time, Vance had seen him. Had they met, worked together, or maybe it was in a mug shot?

When the intruder finally backed to the door, he stepped over his fallen comrade and took a final look at the room. "I got what I came for," he announced. "And it looks like you'll get what you came for as well. Shame about Benny, but it does save me giving him his cut." Flipping the room's light switch off with his elbow, the man stepped into the night.

Vance's first instinct was the chase him, but at the moment there was something far more important to do. He had to make sure the woman he'd been assigned to pick up was all right.

As the Ford started and pulled away from the door, the investigator crept around the room, pulled Benny out of the entry, then closed and locked the door. With that accomplished he once more flipped on the light and turned to face the woman.

"It's all over," he announced hoping she didn't hear his nervousness in his tone. "My name's Dizzy Vance and I've been sent by the President to get you. You've got nothing to fear, I'm going to take you to someplace safe." He noted two crutches standing in a corner. "If I get those for you, can you walk?"

"Yes," she whispered.

He quickly retrieved them. After handing the crutches to Crawford, he turned the man in the bed over and grabbed his wallet from his coat. Vance then repeated the action with Benny. He hoped when he did find time to study the men's identification papers, they would shed some light on what just happened. Cracking the door, he studied the parking lot. A few of the patrons had opened their doors, stepped outside, and were trying to figure out what had just happened. Surprisingly none of them seemed panicked. Perhaps he could use this to his advantage and buy some time.

Slipping his gun into his coat, he stepped out the door and announced, "Sorry for the disturbance, my friend's car backfired a few times. I guess it's that cheap fuel we're getting now."

"I know what you're talking about," one of the men laughed. "Happens to me all the time."

Seemingly satisfied, the trio who'd come out to investigate stole back into their rooms and turned out their lights. Still playing it by ear, Vance reentered the cottage and looked at Crawford.

"I'm going across the road, getting my car, and then I'll pull it right in front of this door. You need to get in as soon as I get here. We need to be well clear of here before anyone finds out what really happened. Do you understand?"

"Yes, sir," she whispered.

Stepping out, Vance hurried across the lot and slid into the Dodge. The starter turned over twice before it caught. He quickly drove across the road, through Eastside's lot, and to the cabin. Crawford, supporting herself on crutches, was waiting for him at the room's open entry. Vance reached across the car and pushed the passenger door open. The woman turned sideways, sat down, and handed him her crutches. The investigator watched as the woman placed her hands under her knees and lifted her almost useless legs into the car. That act accomplished, she hurriedly reached out and closed the door.

"It's going to be okay," he assured her as she slowly pulled from the lot.

And it was going to okay for a while. In spite of all the blood, they'd actually made a pretty clean escape. But tomorrow, when the maid cleaned up that room, things were going to be upside down here. Hopefully by the time everything broke open, Vance and Crawford would be on a plane heading to Maryland and never be connected to the two bodies in that cottage.

As one mile became two and two drifted along to three, Vance was still anything but relaxed. Why had this blown up in his face? Why was anyone murdered? And who was that man he thought he knew but for some reason couldn't remember? The who would haunt him long after he'd pushed the other two unanswered questions into the deep recesses of his mind.

CHAPTER 19

Saturday, July 4, 1942
2:03 p.m.
Team Headquarters outside of Drury, Maryland

Helen Meeker was still scratched and bruised from the bombing she'd survived a week before. From the previous day's wild ride in a flooded creek, Becca Bobbs had a knot on her head and was still dealing with water in her ears. Though not physically injured, Dizzy Vance was still mentally shaken by the firefight he'd somehow survived. But, for the moment, all the mental and physical anguish was worth it. For three victims, personal independence had come on this special anniversary of American independence, but sadly, not for the fourth. Where was she, who had her, and what did this have to do with the prisoner swap requested by Nazi Germany? Until they knew, the team could not rest.

Meeker eased down into one of the living room's Queen Anne chairs and studied her exhausted comrades. Bobbs was huddled in the corner of the couch with her feet tucked up under her body and eyes closed. Vance, a cup of coffee in his right hand, had collapsed into a leather reading chair and was staring at rather than actually reading today's *Post*. Meanwhile, an absent Clay Barnes was still in the field trying to find out why the fourth kidnapping victim was not at the Horseshoe Motor Court in Denton, Texas.

"How's Marge Crawford?" Meeker asked Vance. She actually knew the answer. She'd just checked on the young woman, who they were temporarily boarding in a back room, and found Crawford listening to a radio and reading a magazine. In fact, she might have been in better shape than any of the team members that had made it home. So why had she asked? It was just a way to get a sullen Vance to open up. He'd been as quiet as a church mouse since he'd gotten back.

"She's about as well as can be expected," the investigator quietly explained. "But what kind of future does she really have? What did we save her for? Marge has no one. Her family gave her up when she was seven and turned her over to an orphanage. That's where she grew up. Then that rattrap pushed her out on the streets at eighteen and she's spent her adult years alone. For the last decade, she hasn't gotten a birthday card or a Christmas present. Except for going to Warm Springs a couple of times, all she's had is a job and lousy room. She needs to be needed."

"I know," Meeker agreed.

"Do you?" Vance asked his eyes almost pleading. "Do any of us really know what it's like to grow up thinking you're worth nothing? She needs to be valued for the first time in her whole life." The tough man eyes grew a bit moist as he added, "No one should be alone in a lousy room listening to a radio and cooking on a hotplate. There has to be more to life than that."

Meeker nodded. Vance was right, the story Madge Crawford had lived was one of the saddest she'd heard. In fact, it made the two others they'd rescued seem as if they'd had wonderful lives. Yet, that wasn't really true. When she'd taken Calvin Rawling home, he still couldn't walk. Thus, he had little chance at real independence. The only person who'd likely treat the kid with dignity was his father. Everyone else would likely either pity him or avoid him like the plague.

128

"It was good to get Andrew back to his mother," Bobbs chimed in as if that statement could somehow change the mood. Whatever positive impact she'd made was lost with her next observation. "I just wish he could get into school. He's bright and filled with courage and yet he's isolated."

"But at least he has a mother who loves him," Vance noted.

Meeker sadly nodded. "Was Madge able to tell you what happened?"

"Some," the investigator replied. "Frank Taylor, the man who took her, was the dead guy on the bed. She told me he was nice, polite, and made sure all her needs were met. The billfold I grabbed also proved him to be the Hammond employee who has been assigned to the job. Madge didn't see any other people except for the pair last night. Not long before I got there, two men invaded the room with no warning. Madge said the one that got away obviously knew Frank Taylor. They had an argument over some kind of payoff. It didn't go well for Taylor. Even after he handed the man he called Jock or Jost —Madge didn't get the exact name—a briefcase full of cash, Benny shot him. They were about to leave when I showed up."

"What were they going to do with the girl?" Bobbs asked.

"She thought they were going to kill her," Vance explained. "It seemed Jock didn't want any witnesses."

"What about Benny?" Meeker asked.

"I've done some research. Benny is just one of his names and he has a long record. He was basically a muscle man and spent a couple of stretches in the pen for robbery and assault and battery. Ironically, he worked with Rudy Carfono for a while, but I guess his con days are over now."

Meeker stood, crossed her arms and walked over to the window. Once there she posed another question. "Do you think there was any connection between the kidnapping and the two thugs?"

Vance shrugged. "My gut tells me that they were blackmailing Taylor and the payoff was arranged at the motor court. We'd have to dig into the company files and the man's personal life to find out more about that."

"We'll let the cops do it," Meeker said. "We still have a missing girl to worry about."

She'd just finished her observation when the phone rang. She moved quickly to a table and picked it up.

"HM," she announced.

"It's Clay."

"You got anything?"

"The Boatright girl was picked up by a well-dressed guy who produced FBI identification. He was thin, wore dark glasses, and had an accent. The people I talked to thought he was likely from … get this … either Boston or maybe the British Isles. He got to the motor court about two hours before I arrived. So he knew about the deal and appeared legit."

"Well," she assured him, "he's not. The FBI knows nothing about Amy Boatright getting picked up. I had Alison check."

"How did anyone find out?" Barnes asked.

"I don't see how they could," Meeker explained. "I told the President and the only people he would have shared the information with were trusted staff members."

"Well somebody got wind of this," Barnes noted, "I wonder how?"

"That's the million dollar question. What do you have planned now?"

"The guy who grabbed the girl is long gone," he explained. "I went to the Denton airport and discovered he'd chartered a plane. The deal was done with cash and the pilot's not come back. My guess is he won't. There was a guy at the airport that explained they were going to refuel in Batesville. There are several of those around here. I'm going to start with Arkansas and see what I can dig up. In fact, I'm only about an hour from there right now."

"Keep us informed," Meeker suggested.

"Will do."

Meeker hung up and looked back to the two other team members. After sharing what she'd learned, she waited for suggestions. Sadly there were none. Like Barnes, everyone had hit a dead end. After several awkward moments, Bobbs delivered an insight.

"To find Amy Boatright, we must know who leaked the information."

"Who knew?" Vance demanded. "There was the four of us and Helen told the President."

"Actually," Meeker cut in, "I didn't give the President the locations, so we can rule out a leak at the White House."

"Schmeidler," Bobbs suggested.

Meeker nodded. He and the four men involved in the kidnapping were the only other sources left. But why would any of them tell anyone? It made no sense at all. Picking up the phone, she called her sister.

"I need for you to find out where Harold Schmeidler is today," Meeker barked as soon as the girl answered.

"I can you that right now," Alison explained.

"How?" Meeker demanded.

"Pick up the newspaper or turn on the radio," the younger woman suggested. "Sometime after you left him, he bought a one-way ticket."

"Dead?"

"Murdered. Someone beat him to death."

"Thanks."

Meeker looked back to her team. "The leak was likely mixed with blood. Someone else, likely working with the same information we had, figured out Schmeidler was behind it. They extracted the information the old fashioned way."

"You mean," Bobbs cut it.

The team leader grimly nodded. "He won't have to worry about prosecution now."

"Wasn't the FBI working on the kidnappings?" Vance asked.

"Yeah," Meeker admitted, "they even had the information

before we did. And trying to figure out which one of a few dozen agents is the black sheep will be impossible. Without knowing who that guy is, how do we find the girl?"

Vance snapped his fingers and bolted out of his chair. "Jop!" he exclaimed.

"What?" Bobbs asked.

"The name Madge was trying to remember wasn't Jock, it was Jop. And that's why I know the guy." He licked his lips and shook his head. "Sure there was more than a decade of rough living added, but it was him."

"Who," Meeker demanded.

"Jake Redman," the investigator explained. "He was one of the men I faced down that day on the road when I ..." He paused, frowned and then whispered, "Shot my son."

"You're sure it was him?" Bobbs asked.

Regaining his composure, Vance nodded. "Yeah. Everyone called him Jop because he was from Joplin. This is not a local police matter; this is very personal. I'll get him if it's the last thing I do."

Meeker violently shook her head "There's time for that later. There's a woman who trusts only you right now. She needs to have you help her find a place in life ... someplace that has more than a radio and movie magazines. You can't leave."

"I waited for years to find this guy," he argued. "It drove me to drink. It has my dreams and my nightmares. I can't walk away."

"No buts about this Vance," Meeker shot back, "Revenge is fine in some cases, and I won't argue that you likely deserve it. But you put your desires ahead of your family a long time ago and, I'm sorry I have to remind you of this, but it blew up in your face. Don't do that again. Marge Crawford needs you. Without you she has no one. You saved her; therefore, you can't just walk away."

"So I just let him go?" Vance yelled. "I just let the man who ruined my life and cost me my family walk away?"

"No," Meeker argued, "We will all work with you on getting him. Becca and I will start the ball rolling today. We make sure the FBI's best are involved. The President will do that for us. Then when we find out something, if that is next week or next year, we'll move in together. But right now you need to be with that woman."

"Is that an order?" he demanded.

"Does it have to be?"

Vance rubbed his three chins and frowned. As he did his shoulders slumped and his eyes filled with tears.

"What about it, Dizzy?" Meeker softly asked.

Glancing back to his boss, the man sadly shrugged. "What can we do for her?"

"You're the only one of us who can go out in public. After all, we're supposed to be dead and therefore, we are way undercover. You're not. So, at this moment, Becca and I will work with Clay trying to track down the missing girl and finding clues on Jop, and you will take Madge to see the President."

"What?"

"FDR wants to visit with her and he's found a job for her as well. There's a position for Madge at Warm Springs. So you can take her to the White House. You'll be spending the night there. Imagine what that will mean to that young woman. I really can't think of a better way to celebrate July 4th than that. Can you?"

"Okay," he agreed. "I'll do that much."

"And," Meeker added, "the President needs you drive her to Georgia tomorrow and then spend a few days to make sure security is up to snuff. He wants her to feel safe and he wants to be sure the other patients are as well."

"When do I leave?" he asked.

"As soon as you can; there will be a pass for you at the White House gate. So, why don't you go tell her the news? And drive that 1942 Mercury they just gave us. I'll bet Marge has never ridden in a new car."

Vance forced a smile, stuck his hands in pockets, and

133

exited the room. Once he was gone Bobbs got up and moved to Meeker's side.

"How do we find Amy Boatright?"

"Becca, loose lips sink ships."

"And?"

"As you suggested, we'll have to find out who's talking out of school before we can begin to figure out what happened to the young woman from Oklahoma. So the first question becomes, who else could profit from getting that kid? I mean she's not worth anything in the way of ransom. And we know she's not worth anything to the Germans now."

"Helen, it could only be someone at the FBI looking to get in Hoover's good graces."

Meeker nodded, "That's my first thought as well. If that's the case, then the girl should be returned unharmed. She's only good for brownie points if she's healthy and alive."

"That's rings true," Bobbs agreed.

"So," Meeker suggested, "Let's change our focus. Rather than look for Amy Boatright, let's see who's on Hoover's bad list right now. I'm going to need to put Alison to work on that."

"Then what do I do?" Bobbs asked.

"You find out what's going on with the investigation in Indiana. Make a few calls and see if the cops know why there was a payoff, why the man watching Crawford was murdered, and what happened to Jop."

"Got it," Bobbs announced as she turned to walk out of the room. When she got to the door, she stopped and turned back to the other woman. "Helen, the guy who picked up the Boatright girl is in Texas."

"So," Meeker suggested, "you're thinking what I'm thinking."

"He's dead," Bobbs pointed out.

"So are we."

"You don't actually believe it."

"No," Meeker assured her friend, "I don't. But I'm not

ruling it out either. After all, we know that Alistar died, but we still don't know what happened to Reggie. And if that was him in Denton, Texas, then which side is he really on?"

CHAPTER 20

Saturday, July 4, 1942
5:00 p.m.
A small farm outside of Springfield, Illinois

Fredrick Bauer, wearing a white wig, fake beard, and glasses, sat on a stool placed beside one of his examining tables adjusting a screw on the side of a stainless steel brace. He studied the results, smiled, and twisted a small knob one notch forward. He happily observed the brace move ninety degrees. After placing it on the table beside what looked like its mirror twin, he looked from his work to his guest.

A confused Amy Boatright was sitting on that same table next to the braces. The teenager was about five feet tall and likely weighed no more than ninety-five pounds. She had fair skin, dark eyes, and light brunette hair. Though obviously frightened, her concern couldn't hide the fact she was the picture of All-American cute.

"I don't understand," she whispered. Her voice was soft, lilting, and carried a heavy Oklahoma twang. "Why did you bring me here? And why was I blindfolded when I came?"

"This lab's secret," Bauer gently explained. "And don't worry, you won't be here for long. Within a day or so you'll be back at your mother's house. But I don't want to see you reunited with her until I give you a present."

"I still don't understand."

He nodded.

Bauer normally controlled people through fear, but, in this case, that option was off the table. He didn't want to traumatize the girl; he actually wanted to help her. Moving closer he tried to explain.

"I've been working on braces like this for a long time. You see, I once knew a child that got infantile paralysis. I started this research hoping to help him. He died before I could finish. These braces setting on table ..." Bauer stopped, ran his hand over the brace nearest the girl and smiled. When he again picked up the conversation, his voice cracked with emotion. "Amy, these braces are the result of that work. I've adjusted them for your size. Let's put them on."

"But," she protested.

"If you don't like them," he explained, "you don't have to keep them."

"Okay, I'll try them. If I do this, then can I go home?"

"Absolutely."

Bauer picked one up and began to fit the brace onto her right leg. When he finished, he locked the brace into a sitting position. He then repeated the action on the left side.

"How do they feel?" he asked.

"Pretty much like the ones they gave me at Warm Springs," she said. "And I don't use those much. They're too hard to put on. I usually just kind of drag myself around with my crutches or scoot on the floor."

He sadly nodded. That was no way for a person live. No one should be in a world where they couldn't be mobile.

"As you can see," Bauer explained, "these just snap on in three places. So they are easy to put on. When you want them off, you push one button and the latches unlock." He demonstrated how the buttons worked. "Now, just put them back together like this and they snap in place."

"That's easy," she admitted, "but they're still braces. It's not like I can walk."

"They're really a bit more than that," he assured her. "Do you see that each has a small knob on the outside of the knee?" Boatright scanned the right one and nodded.

"Right now it's in the sitting position, but watch what happens when I move the knob one notch forward. Now don't be frightened, just let the brace do what it's meant to do." After one click, the right brace, on its own moved the bottom half of Boatright's leg upward until it was straight. Bauer waited a bit for the girl to get used to the new angle before explaining. "This is the standing position. Let me move the other one to the same place and we will get you off this table."

Stepping over quickly to Boatright's left side, he moved the knob once notch forward. Two seconds later, when it was in place, he put his hands under the young woman's arms and lifted her off the table to the floor. After allowing her to gain her balance, he stepped away.

Boatright looked down at the twin braces currently locked over her slacks. Once she realized what she was doing, she laughed. Fifteen seconds later, she whispered, "I'm standing without crutches."

"And that's a start," Bauer assured her. "But now you're going to do something else without crutches." He pointed to a bookcase on a nearby wall. "How far would you say that is from us?"

"Maybe fifteen feet," came the quick reply.

"Okay," he announced, "find those knobs I turned to put you in a standing position and move each of them to the last notch. That will be the position all the way to the front."

She bent at her waist and twisted the right knob. Nothing happened. She then repeated the action on the left with the same result. Straightening up she shrugged.

"What's it supposed to do?"

ACE COLLINS

Bauer moved away from the table to a point halfway between Boatright and the bookcase. "Okay, slowly move your right leg forward."

"I can't," she argued.

"No," he argued, "you couldn't. But now you can. Just try it."

She cautiously pushed her right leg three inches forward. The knee bent just like a real leg and then popped back into place. Boatright grinned. She moved the left in the same way.

"That's right," he assured her. "Don't bite off too much. But the springs in the braces will allow you to walk. It won't be as smooth as a normal person's gate, but just keep coming toward me."

One step led to another and then another and the three-inch stride became five and then nine. As she moved closer, Bauer stepped to one side and watched her complete her trip to the bookcase. Her smile could have lit the room as she put her hands on one of the books she found there.

After slowly turning, with the book still her hand, she said, "I can't believe it."

"You'll get better," he assured her. "You're not going to run with them, but you will be able to get from place to place now a lot more effectively than you ever have before. Just think of this, when you see your mother the next time, you will walk into her arms."

"I'm going to walk back to the table," Boatright announced.

"That's fine," Bauer said. "But don't go to fast. You've not learned much about balance yet. If you hurry, you will probably fall. In fact, before we leave, I will give you a cane to help you some."

"Okay."

Moving back to the stool, the disguised man laughed when Boatright finished her second trip. She might have been back to where she started, but in truth she had just traveled a very long way in a short amount of time and space.

"Let's give you an hour of walking," he suggested. "Then I'm going to take you to a place where the FBI will pick you up. After that, you'll be able to go home."

She looked up and, with tears in her eyes, smiled. "Thank you, sir."

Bauer nodded and turned his face toward the wall. He was misting up and no one, not even a young, innocent girl, was allowed to see that he actually had a heart.

CHAPTER 21

Saturday, July 4, 1942
10:31 p.m.
A roadside picnic area off Highway
34 ten miles east of Covington, Indiana

Teresa Bryant delivered the news on Amy Boatright to J. Edgar Hoover late Friday afternoon. She explained there had to be a woman present when the exchange was made or it was no deal. She then convinced the director she was the best woman for the job. Hoover only agreed to let Bryant go if James Killpatrick accompanied her. She was going to insist on Killpatrick going if the director hadn't, so the director's orders fit perfectly into her plans.

Bryant and Killpatrick flew from Washington to Chicago where they picked up another agent and an FBI-owned 1940 Buick. They then drove the vehicle to Danville, Illinois, where they stopped at a roadside diner for supper. It was just past nine-thirty when they finished the meal, paid the bill and left. Very little was said until they drove through the quaint Indiana town of Covington. By this time, most of its two thousand twenty-six citizens were asleep.

It was Killpatrick who broke the silence asking a question

he'd already posed a dozen times. "How did you find out what my team couldn't?"

Bryant, dressed in black slacks and matching sweater, shrugged from the passenger side of the huge car's front seat. Killpatrick had never excited her and now he was really starting to get on her nerves.

"Give!" the agent demanded.

"How many times do you have to ask that question?"

The driver growled, "Until I get an answer."

"I've given you answers," she barked. "I made the right calls."

"Just leave her alone," Chet Morris begged from the backseat. "If this plays out as planned, then we'll all look like heroes. So who cares where the lead came from?"

"Thank you, Chet," Bryant cooed. She glanced back to the tall, thin agent, who looked a bit like Jimmy Stewart, and smiled. Morris was a good guy. She'd enjoyed visiting with him on the trip. She was also pretty sure he knew much more about how to treat a lady than did the driver.

"Okay," a frustrated Killpatrick noted, "we're coming up to the drop spot. Let's go over how we handle this."

"We pull up to the picnic spot," Morris explained. "I stay in the car with my gun ready and my eyes open. The two of you get out, walk up a hill to a clump of five sycamores. The girl should be waiting at the table. Supposedly no one will be with her. Then you come back to the car with the victim and we drive onto Indy. There we catch a plane to Oklahoma and take the girl home."

"I don't want anyone straying from that plan," Killpatrick warned. "And remember, I'm in charge."

Bryant looked at her watch. They'd been warned not to be early. They weren't. It was already five minutes past the assigned time. If everything worked as planned, she was going to have made a deep inroad into becoming a trusted member of Hoover's team and she would not ever have to kiss up to Killpatrick again.

"Should be somewhere around here," Killpatrick announced

as he looked at the speedometer's mileage counter. We are at the nine-mile point right now."

"There's a hill with a stand of trees just to your right," Morris pointed out. "There's also a lane to pull off into."

Bryant glanced up to the trees. The tops were bathed with what little moonlight there was, but there was no way see under the branches. While she was confident in her source and was sure the girl was there, it would take walking up that lane to verify it. The pickup point was, therefore, perfect. Now it was time to scope out the rest of the layout.

There was a cornfield to the left and somewhere on the other side of that field was a road where a car was waiting. On the right, about fifty feet from the lane leading to the picnic grounds, was another stand of trees surrounded by bushes. Everything was just as advertised.

As Killpatrick pulled the car off the road and killed the engine, Bryant grabbed the handle and opened her door. She had just stepped out onto the gravel when Killpatrick rounded the car's nose. In the back seat, Morris placed a rifle on top of the rear door's window opening and got ready for action.

"Hope I don't have to use this," the man noted.

Killpatrick nodded. "So do I. Remember Teresa, I'm in charge here. You don't lead; you follow me. Now let's go up that hill. And keep your eyes open, it could be a trap."

Though he didn't pull it out, simply by his posture anyone would have known the agent was squeezing a gun hidden in his pocket. Bryant grimly smiled, so much for the promise to come unarmed.

Due to Killpatrick's deliberate pace, it took the pair almost a minute to move across the open hill to a point under the trees. Thanks to the shade blocking the moonlight, it was now so dark Bryant could now barely see the agent just three feet ahead. Thus, when he abruptly stopped, she banged into him.

"Watch where you're going," he grumbled. "I can't see a blasted thing."

"Then use your flashlight," the woman suggested.

She waited as Killpatrick pulled the flashlight from his left pocket, pushed the button, and directed the beam under the trees. Sitting all alone at a table was a young woman dressed in slacks and a light jacket. The sudden appearance of the light caused her to throw up her hands in front of her face, but surprisingly, she still appeared very calm.

"Amy Boatright?" Killpatrick barked.

"Yes," she assured him. "Are you with the FBI?"

"We are," he answered as he quickly moved forward. Sitting the flashlight on the table's top where it lit the girl's face, Killpatrick studied the victim. As he did, Bryant walked around the table to Boatright's side.

"You ready to go home?"

"Yes, ma'am."

"Do you need any helped?" Bryant asked.

"No," Boatright assured the woman, "I can do this."

Swinging around the wooden eight by two board serving as the table's bench, Boatright reached down and twisted knobs on both braces. As she did, the support devices straightened out. Pushing off the table with her hands, she stood, steadied herself and asked, "Which way do we go?"

"Right down that hill," Bryant noted.

"Will you walk beside me?" Boatright asked.

"Sure, and Agent Killpatrick can follow behind. I'm sure he won't mind."

"Just get going," Killpatrick growled.

Bryant, her eyes now accustomed to the dark, studied the agent. He wasn't even pretending to follow the plan now. His gun was out and ready, but it wasn't going to do him any good.

"You sure that's a good idea?" Bryant asked as she pointed to the weapon. "That was not in the instructions and I'd hate for someone to take offense at us now."

"We've got the kid," he shot back, "so now I make the rules."

"Fine," she announced as she turned, placed her hand on the girl's shoulder and took the first steps toward the car. They'd covered about five yards and had just emerged from the trees when Bryant heard a click to her left: she neither stopped nor turned. A second, later the row of bushes she'd noted earlier erupted with machinegun fire. Instinct told the woman to run, but experience held her in place. With her hand still on Boatright, Bryant continued her slow trek down the hill.

The blast was short and precise. The thirty or so rounds that were fired all went behind the two women. Byrant didn't have to look back to know what they hit. Now there was one less set of footsteps.

Looking down to the Buick, Bryant noted Morris aim his rifle toward the underbrush. He quickly squeezed off three rounds and then waited for a reply. There was none.

As the women continued to move toward the car, Boatright leaned close to Bryant and whispered, "I can't run. What do I do?"

"Just keeping walking," came the calm reply.

"But the gunfire?"

"We don't have to worry about that," Bryant assured her. "The bullets found what they were looking for."

As Bryant and Boatright moved deliberately forward, Morris got out the car, and, rifle in hand, rushed up to them.

"Where's Jimmy?"

Bryant quickly answered, "Back there in the shadows, but there's no use checking on him."

Morris glanced toward the bushes looking for movement. There was none. He then turned his gaze back toward the top of the hill.

"I see him on the ground," the man announced. "I'll check on him after I get you two in the car."

With Morris walking backwards, his gun pointing toward the place where they'd all seen and heard the machine gun fire, Bryant glanced over to Boatright and with a calm voice noted,

"We'll get into the car and you'll be safe. Just keep moving forward." A minute later they were beside the Buick.

"I'm going to check on Jimmy," Morris announced, "and then I'll have a look at the place where they fired from."

"We'll wait in the car," Bryant suggested. "Don't take too long. And don't worry about the bushes, whoever shot Killpatrick is likely gone."

"How do you know?" the agent demanded.

"Just a hunch," came the unemotional reply.

As Morris raced up the hill, Bryant helped Boatright into the backseat. Only after the young woman adjusted her braces did the FBI's newest employee join her.

"Miss …"

"Call me Teresa."

"Teresa, what happened back there?"

"A FBI agent got shot," Bryant explained, "but it had nothing to do with you. It was just someone settling a score. By the way, what was the man like who brought you here?"

"He was kind of good looking, in a rugged sort of way," she explained. "He didn't talk much, but when he did, he sounded like he was from England. He also called my mother 'mum.' That was kind of strange. He wasn't warm like the old man who made these new braces for me."

"An old man?" Bryant asked.

"Yeah, he was tall and thin."

Okay, that likely meant Bauer had worn a disguise and made the braces, but why hadn't he brought the girl to the drop-off point? There was no one else there when she visited the farm the other night. Surely it couldn't be …

A suddenly shaky Bryant turned her gaze back to the hill. Morris was emerging from the bushes shaking his head. "No one back there," he called out.

"Not surprised," the woman shouted out the window.

Returning to the car, the agent looked through the open back window. As if in disbelief he whispered, "Jimmy's dead."

Bryant grimly smiled. Killpatrick had gotten in too deep. He'd play both sides of the street too long. Besides she didn't need him anymore. It was amazing how fast this was all coming together. Still, there was one troubling aspect that reared its head tonight. If the gunman who got Killpatrick was who she thought it was, then she wasn't the only ghost in this game.

CHAPTER 22

Monday, July 6, 1942
Midnight
A rowboat one mile off the Dover coast

Henry Reese knew he was taking a big chance. He was basing a strategic move on information gained from Nigel Armstrong. If what Armstrong shared was confirmed, Reese would be making a long trip in a U-boat. If the captured spy had lied, then this was a suicide mission.

Dressed completely in black, the former FBI agent waited in the small, wooden boat and studied the calm English Channel waters. He was at the right location, the rendezvous time was now, so where was the sub? Five minutes stretched to ten and ten to twenty and still no ride. Finally, at thirty minutes past the hour, the American noted a periscope slicing the water to his right. Reese took out his flashlight and turned it on and off three times. Five minutes later U-Boat 1037 appeared. It had no more than cleared the surface when four men scrambled onto the conning tower. Reese flashed three more times and began rowing over to the sub.

"Mr. Armstrong?" a voice called out.

"Yes," Reese assured him. "Do you have my payoff?"

"We do," came the reply. "Come aboard."

It took five minutes to row to the Nazi submarine, climb onto the deck, up to the tower, and down the hatch. Once inside the visitor was led back through the cramped passageways and stations to the commanding officer's cabin. Sitting beside a bunk was a trunk.

"Your payoff is in there," the commander announced. "My name is Klein. Feel free to open it and examine the contents."

The American's eyes went from the trunk to the small room Klein called home. The walls were lined with wooden paneling. The furniture consisted of a desk, a bunk, and a filing cabinet. A storage locker likely held the officer's clothing. This was definitely not a place to entertain guests.

"It's modest," Klein said with a degree of pride, "but it's home. I hope you aren't claustrophobic."

"I'm not," Reese assured him. "And about the box, why don't you open it."

The commander smiled. "You don't trust us. I'm guessing you think it might be booby-trapped."

"I trust no one," came the cocky reply. "In this game, when you trust people you die."

Klein leaned down and flipped two latches. Grabbing the top, he opened the lid. The box was filled with American cash, diamonds, and a few gold bars. Looking back to his guest, the German asked, "What do you think?"

"Christmas shopping just got a lot easier," Reese announced.

"So," Klein noted as he closed the trunk, "I guess we are on our way to South America."

"No, I've changed my mind. I want to go to Mexico."

Reaching inside his pocket, Reese pulled out a map and handed it to Klein. The German looked it over and shrugged. "It will be a slightly shorter trip."

"Which means," the American noted, "you'd be hunting big fish again much sooner than if we went that far south."

The commander looked at a calendar. "Based on how far

we'll have to go, I can likely drop you off on the night of July 19th."

"Just as I figured," Reese answered. "When we are one day from landing I'll have you send out a coded message to my contact. Now, where do I stay?"

"Follow me," Klein announced. "I'm short an officer on this outing, so you can have his bunk. As we won't be hunting, it should be an uneventful trip."

"Let's hope so."

The commander led Reese down a hallway and into another small room with four bunks. He pointed to the one on the top right. "That's yours. Anything else you need?"

"No," came the reply.

"And what about the name you are to give me?"

"When I am safely on the beach in Mexico."

"I'll keep the trunk in my office until then," Klein announced. He then nodded and left.

Tossing a small duffle back onto his bed, Reese exhaled deeply. So far so good! Armstrong had assured him that no one knew him on the sub and that information had so far proven reliable. Now it was time to sit back and relax.

CHAPTER 23

Helen Meeker was standing on the home's front porch enjoying a beautiful summer morning when Becca Bobbs joined her.

"Smell the roses," Meeker suggested.

"Maybe later," Bobbs answered. "What's up?"

"Alison called about seven. She's been working all night on gathering some stuff for us. Apparently, at least a part of what she found was too sensitive to deliver over the phone."

"Any clue as to what it could be?"

"None," Meeker admitted, "but we should know soon. Her car just entered the front gate. So be ready to translate for me."

"Got it," Bobbs laughed.

As the 1936 Packard drove down the long lane, Meeker and Bobbs walked to the edge of the walk and to the driveway. After stepping out of the car, Alison hugged her sister and extended a wrapped package toward Bobbs. As Meeker looked on, both the other women laughed.

"What's that?" Meeker demanded.

"Just something for a platterbug," Alison replied.

"A platterbug?"

Bobbs explained. "A platterbug is someone who loves to listen to records." She then turned back to the visitor? "Skinny blue eyes, balding crooner, or slide king?"

"Slide king," Alison assured her. "I'm hep on what your tongue wants and it sure wasn't the tintype."

"I'm lost," Meeker admitted.

Her sister groaned. "Can't you follow even the simplest score?"

"I guess not."

"She asked me if the wax was Sinatra, Crosby, or Glen Miller."

"What about the tintype?"

"Sis, that's code for an old person. Crosby is prehistoric. After all, he's like thirty-nine."

"Right," Meeker answered. "I'll make a note of that. Now, why the trip?"

"Wheels are safer than wires," Alison explained. "Let's go to the dining car and I'll make with the crash course."

"You're hungry?" Meeker asked.

"Didn't have time to shake up some eggs this morning."

"Okay, sis, you lead the way."

After arriving at the kitchen, Alison pulled out a chair and sat at a small, wooden kitchen table. Meanwhile, Bobbs became, what Alison called a hash slinger.

"So," Meeker suggested, "while we wait for Betty Crocker, why don't you give us an update on Boatright. And please do it in English."

The visitor frowned. "Fine. She's on the up and up and has a new set of braces that are out of this world. They are so out there, the President wants a set of them."

"Where'd she get them?" Bobbs called out from the stove.

"From some old man. She has no idea who he was, but he did share he had started his research because someone he loved had polio. And he wasn't the guy who picked her up. That guy talked like Churchill."

"A Brit?" Meeker asked.

Alison shrugged. "Hoover figures it was someone sounding British to throw the hounds off the trail."

"I understand," Meeker chimed in, "James Killpatrick died when they picked up the kid."

"He played catcher and lost," Alison explained. "A tommy gun filled him with enough lead to make some pretty heavy barbells. It was all the more bizarre because two other G-men types were there and the shooter didn't even fire at them. So old J. Edgar thinks it had nothing to do with the kidnapping, just someone out to settle a score with Killpatrick." She paused and looked at her sister. "Was that plain enough for you?"

"Yes, I appreciate not having to go through a translator. Still, it doesn't sound like you needed to drive all this way to tell us that."

"No," she admitted. "That's not the reason for playing Lewis and Clark. I'll give you this to you on the level so Becca doesn't have to translate. The OSS got a strange message the other night. They sent it through a lot of different code experts and they struck out. It ended up on the President's desk, I looked at it and knew exactly what it said."

Bobbs slipped the eggs and three strips of bacon onto a plate and waltzed over to the table. After sitting the food in front of the hungry guest, she asked, "How did you know and they didn't?"

"They're like Helen," Alison noted, "they're about two decades behind the scene." She took a bite of eggs and smiled. "Becca, these are on the square."

"Thank you. Now, what about the code?"

"It's a language all of us kids are using. We call it Opish. You take the first letter and put it at the end of the word and then ad 'op' after that. So 'Helen rules' would become, 'elenhopulesrop.' And there are no spaces. You never take a breath while saying it."

Bobbs nodded. "Okay, let me try this. Avehopouopadopnyaopatesdop-ecentlyreop?"

"Aldlyoponop."

Meeker waved her hands and demanded, "Translate."

"Becca wanted to know if I'd had any dates recently and I told that sadly I hadn't. The one guy who asked me I turned down because he was droopy and I'm looking for a real cuddle cat so I'm not taking in strays. Most of the cats a gal would consider muzzle-nuzzling are working for uncle."

Ignoring what she didn't understand, Meeker plunged forward on what she actually felt she had to know. "And what was in the message that was translated for the president?"

"Do you want me to give it to you in Opish or English?"

"English."

Alison shrugged. "That's hardly using your Disney."

"What?"

"Never mind, the message was, 'Have Helen and her team ready to pick up a package in Tampico, Mexico, between the 18th and 21st to be delivered by U-boat."

"And the President doesn't know what this means?" Bobbs asked.

"He's either not clued in," Alison admitted, "or he's not giving with the goods. Might be a bit of both. He likes to yank my chain. He did tell me you'll receive more instructions the day before the pickup and you might need firepower. Oh, and in a few days a visitor from England will be here to be a part of that mission. I'm guessing she must have the mental files you need to draw the whole picture."

"Great," Meeker groaned, "another person to babysit."

"And," Alison added, "hisopillopebophristmascopnoiopulyjop."

"He really said that?" Bobbs asked.

"No," the younger woman admitted, "at least not in Opish. But that was the song he was singing."

"I'm still lost," Meeker groaned.

"Stir the stew," Alison suggested, "it will come to you."

158

Bobbs shrugged. "What could we receive that would make it Christmas in July?"

"Is that what that meant?" Meeker asked.

"Yep," her sister said as the phone rang.

"I'll get it," Bobbs announced.

As the blonde took the message and Alison finished her breakfast, Meeker considered the news. A U-boat rarely brought anything but destruction, so how could it deliver a present she'd want? Besides, in a situation like this, why not send in the Navy and the Army Air Corps?

Bobbs put down the phone and snapped her fingers to grab everyone's attention. "Helen, that was Clay, he has a lead on the water source. He's now traced it back to Arkansas. He doesn't have a location, but he's staying on the trail."

"Fine," Meeker noted.

"Oh," Alison added as she finished up the last bite of bacon, "there's one more thing."

Meeker turned to face her sister. "What's that?"

"You're supposed to find out who made a pincushion out of Killpatrick. As the FBI is striking out, it seems that this might be an inside job. If that is the case the only way to unmask the mole is from the outside in."

"Dizzy's due back in a day," Meeker explained. "He'll love that assignment and maybe it'll keep his mind off trying to find Jop."

"What a Jop?" Alison asked.

"Human mud ball," Bobbs explained.

"Got it," the younger woman said.

As the other two other women began a discourse on hot platters and cool crooners, Meeker stepped out of the kitchen and strolled down the hall to her war room. It might be about a week and a half away, but being a welcoming committee for a Nazi U-boat was going to take some planning. Then there was the matter of Killpatrick. Why was he taken out and where did she begin the search for his killer? And these two mysterious items didn't even touch the other things already on her plate. What about the water and the missing documents? And who punched Carfono's ticket and why? And then there was man Vance wanted to find; so far that trail was dead. And then there was Reggie Fister—had he changed sides or was the man in Texas a new pawn in this complicated chess match?

Don't forget the previous episodes ...
In the President's Service Series.

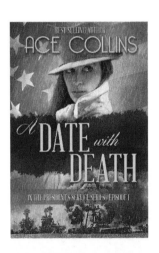

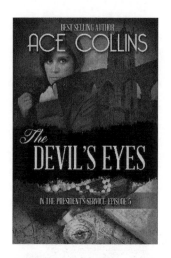

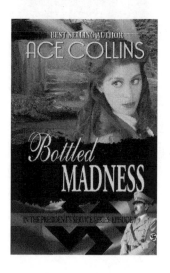

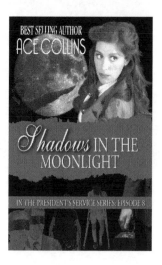

More from Ace Collins.

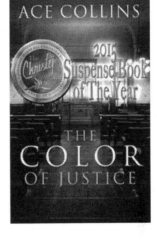

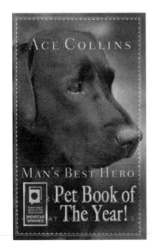

Made in the USA
Middletown, DE
31 July 2017